Praise for Elin Hilderbrand's
WINTER STORMS

"A series only works when the characters are worth following over the long haul, and Hilderbrand is a master."
—*Kirkus Reviews*

"Hilderbrand expertly meshes everything together so that peace exists within each character and within the family dynamic.... The queen of the romance novel is on top of her game, and she won't let you down."
—Vivian Payton, *Bookreporter*

"A perfect mix of love, tears, and joy."
—Kathleen Gerard, *Shelf Awareness*

"Dishy and readable... with some luxurious details adding a touch of glamour to the drama."
—Susan Maguire, *Booklist*

"A beautifully written work that is also engrossing."
—Lauren DuBois, *RT Book Reviews*

"A must-read for any bibliophile who loves a good family drama. You'll laugh, you'll cry, you'll nod your head in agreement... and then you'll settle in to reread the whole damn thing again." —Ashley Macey, *Brit + Co*

ALSO BY ELIN HILDERBRAND

WINTER STORMS
A NOVEL

Elin Hilderbrand

Little, Brown and Company

New York   Boston   London

Copyright © 2016 by Elin Hilderbrand
Excerpt from *Winter Solstice* © 2017 by Elin Hilderbrand

Little, Brown and Company
Hachette Book Group
1290 Avenue of the Americas, New York, NY 10104
littlebrown.com

Little, Brown and Company is a division of Hachette Book Group, Inc. The Little, Brown and Company name and logo is a trademark of Hachette Book Group, Inc.

The publisher is not responsible for websites (or their content) that are not owned by the publisher.

Printed in the United States of America

Originally published in hardcover by Little, Brown and Company, October 2016
First trade paperback edition, October 2017
First Little, Brown and Company mass market edition, September 2018

OPM

10 9 8 7 6 5 4 3 2 1

*For my "little" brother, Douglas
Clarence Hilderbrand, the weatherman*

SPRING

MARGARET

Here is a little-known fact about Margaret Quinn: She likes some news stories better than others. At the bottom of her list are terrorist attacks, random shootings, and...the election. Margaret has to fight off her indifference on a daily basis. She has been on familiar terms with the past three presidents and her overwhelming emotion toward them wasn't awe or admiration, it was pity. Being president of the United States is the most stressful, thankless job in the world and Margaret can't fathom why anyone would voluntarily pursue it. End of topic.

Margaret's favorite kind of news story is—would anyone believe this?—the weather. The dull, the prosaic, the default I-have-nothing-else-to-talk-about-so-let's-talk-about-the-weather topic is, to Margaret's mind, a stunning daily phenomenon, overlooked and taken for granted. Margaret loves it all: hurricanes, tornadoes, blizzards, lightning storms, and—the ultimate bonanza—an earthquake followed by a tsunami. This may seem sadistic, but even as she mourns any loss of life, she is intrigued by the science of it. Weather is a physical manifestation of the earth's power. Margaret also likes that weather defies prediction. Meteorologists can get close, but there are no guarantees.

The world, Margaret thinks, is full of surprises.

*   *   *

Margaret's ex-husband, Kelley Quinn, has prostate cancer. He was diagnosed just before Christmas, which made for another muted, maudlin holiday. Margaret was tempted to take a leave of absence from the network in order to manage Kelley's care, but Kelley's estranged wife, Mitzi, returned to the fold and is now very much in charge. After twenty years of barely concealed animosity, Margaret and Mitzi have come to a place of peace, bordering on friendship, and Margaret would like to keep it that way—so she's backed off. She gets updates every day or two from her daughter, Ava. Kelley's cancer is contained; it hasn't metastasized. He has been traveling back and forth to the Cape five days a week for his radiation treatments. Mitzi goes with him most days, although she's made no secret of the fact that she finds the radiation aggressive. She would prefer Kelley to treat his cancer holistically with herbs, kale smoothies, massage, energy work, and sleep.

Margaret bites her tongue.

One thing that Margaret knows will make both Kelley and Mitzi feel better is getting definitive news about their son, Bart, who has been missing in Afghanistan since December of 2014. Margaret checks her computer first thing each morning for briefs from the DoD. One soldier from Bart's platoon, William Burke, escaped to safety, but he remains at Walter Reed in Bethesda. He sustained life-threatening head trauma and, hence, the DoD has no new intelligence about where the rest of the troops are, or even if they're alive.

But they might soon, Margaret guesses. Assuming the kid makes it.

The winter months are mild, a welcome change from the year before, and spring arrives right on time in the second half of March. It's not a false spring either, but a real, true spring, the kind portrayed in picture books—with bunny rabbits, budding trees, children on swing sets. Margaret's apartment overlooks Central Park and by the first of April, the park is a lush green carpet accented by bursts of color— beds of tulips, daffodils, hyacinths, iris. Model yachts skim across Conservatory Pond. There are soaking rain showers at night so that in the morning when Margaret steps out of her apartment building and into the waiting car, driven by Raoul, the city looks shellacked and the air feels scrubbed clean.

It's a good spring. Kelley will be fine, Margaret tells her-self. Their son Patrick is set to be released from jail on the first of June. He already has a handful of investors and he plans to open his own boutique investment firm. How he managed this from inside the lockup, Margaret isn't sure. She made him promise her that, from here on out, everything he does will be legal.

Margaret's granddaughter, Genevieve, is growing and changing each day. She can now sit up, and technology is so advanced that when Margaret and Kevin connect on Face-Time, Margaret can wave and coo and watch Genevieve laugh. Kevin and Isabelle are busy with the inn, which, thanks to the clement weather, has been filled to capacity since the middle of March.

But what is really painting Margaret's world pink is that she's in love. Dr. Drake Carroll has changed from a some-time lover to her constant companion, best friend, and fiancé. They'd both vowed to make time for the relationship to grow. Margaret had wondered if she would be able to keep her promise, and then she'd wondered if Drake would be able to keep *his*—but she has been pleasantly surprised at how organic and natural it is to be part of a couple again.

Weeknights, they stay at Margaret's apartment, and weekends, they're at Drake's. They go out to dinner downtown at places picked by Margaret's assistant, Darcy, who is a wizard at finding the most fun and delicious spots in the city—the Lion, Saxon and Parole, Jeffrey's Grocery, Uncle Boons. They've been to the theater three times, and they work out side by side at the gym; on Sundays, they order in Vietnamese food and watch old movies. Drake sends Margaret flowers at the studio; he writes *I love you* in soap on the bathroom mirror. Margaret is besotted. When you're in love, every day is like a present you get to open.

Margaret's daughter, Ava, wants to take a trip, just the two of them, before Margaret gets married. It will be a bachelorette trip to celebrate the end of Margaret's freedom! Ava says.

Margaret is lukewarm on the idea. The last thing she needs at her age is a bachelorette celebration. She harks back to a very drunken night nearly forty years earlier that found her roaming the West Village with her six bridesmaids. Alison, the leader of Margaret's bachelorette foray, had insisted they stop at a bar to hear acoustic guitar music and then further insisted that Margaret join the singer—a very cute guy with shoulder-length hair and a naughty gleam in his eye—onstage to sing "American Pie." Margaret impressed the crowd and the band so much with her voice and her knowledge of the lyrics that she got a standing ovation, and the lead singer asked if he could take her home.

No, Margaret had said. She had been genuinely confused. *I'm the one getting married.*

Obviously any trip with Ava would be a far cry from that, but at her age, even the word *bachelorette* makes Margaret cringe.

But one day, as she's kicking it up a notch on the treadmill, Margaret is struck by a realization. This trip Ava is suggesting isn't for Margaret—it's for Ava.

Her daughter needs her.

AVA

Using her mother's credit card and her mother's assistant, Darcy—who has an inexplicably deep reservoir of general knowledge, considering her young age—Ava books five nights in adjoining ocean-view suites at the Malliouhana resort in Anguilla over her spring break.

She needs to get off the island of Nantucket.

Her love life is in a state of emergency.

Through the winter and into the spring, she has been unable to choose between Nathaniel and Scott and so she dates them both. Has anyone on God's green planet ever successfully dated two men at once? Oh yeah? Well, how about on an island that is thirteen miles long and four miles wide? One night, when Ava was out with Scott at a romantic dinner at Company of the Cauldron, Nathaniel walked by outside, saw Ava, and started waving like a madman. He then proceeded to take a lengthy phone call right outside the window, directly in Ava's line of sight. Ava wanted Nathaniel to leave so she could finish her dinner with Scott in peace, but she also wanted to know who Nathaniel was on the phone with. He seemed to be laughing pretty hard. Another time, when Ava was with Nathaniel at Cisco Brewers having a Winter Shredder and listening to the Four Easy Payments, Scott walked in with Roxanne Oliveria, aka Mz. Ohhhhhh, who still had a slight limp from breaking her ankle in December.

Scott said, "Hi, Ava."

Roxanne said, "Oh, hello, Ava."

Ava sipped her Shredder and said nothing. Nathaniel raised a hand to Scott and said, "Hey there, Scotty boy," in a tone of voice that announced his victory. Roxanne smiled at Ava in a way that announced her victory, and then she requested "Brown-Eyed Girl," a choice Ava found over-played and obvious. Ava bumped knees with Nathaniel under the table, and although he certainly wanted to stay and make Scott uncomfortable, he asked for the check.

Ava has told Nathaniel and Scott that she is dating both of them, and she makes it clear they are free to date other people. Nathaniel says he has no interest in anyone but Ava. This is an effective strategy, especially since Ava has had trust issues with Nathaniel in the past and has, on occasion, questioned his devotion. On nights when Ava goes out with Scott, Nathaniel either stops in at the Bar with his crew or stays home and reads Harlan Coben novels; he always texts her when he's hitting the hay. When Ava is out with Nathaniel, Scott goes out with Roxanne. This is also an effective strategy. Ava suspected that Roxanne was making a play for Scott, but she'd never believed Scott would fall for it. When Ava is at school, she will sometimes see Roxanne emerging from the main office wearing one of her low-cut blouses and a tight pencil skirt and absurd wedge heels. Roxanne teaches English at the high school—two buildings away—and there is no reason why she should be at the elementary school except to lean over Scott's desk and let her long hair fall into her cleavage. Ava can't believe the superintendent hasn't spoken to Roxanne about the provocative way she dresses, and Ava can't believe Roxanne still insists on wearing heels even after she's broken her ankle on the cobblestones of Federal Street. Ava's real problem, however, is jealousy. She is insanely jealous of Roxanne. Roxanne is beautiful and alluring; the wedge heels make her calves look amazing. Roxanne has also, apparently, revealed her vulnerable side to Scott, something he is unable to resist. Roxanne has been through three broken engagements—Fiancé One was gay, Fiancé Two was a cheater, and Fiancé Three died in a surfing accident while on vacation in San Diego. Roxanne's loss of the third fiancé leaves Ava unable to hate her. Scott confided to her that Roxanne still sees a therapist to cope with Gunner's death, and she bursts into tears over strange things—orange sunsets, the smell of lily of the valley, the song "Last Nite" by the Strokes.

Both Nathaniel and Scott have been available and supportive for Ava throughout Bart's continued absence and Kelley's illness. Nathaniel is better at *doing* things—he is the one who picks up Kelley and Mitzi from the boat or the airport after radiation; he is the one who wakes up early every day to check the DoD website to see if William Burke has made any medical progress or if any other troops from Bart's platoon have escaped. Scott is better at talking—he asks Ava how she feels about Kelley's illness (although outwardly optimistic, inwardly she's terrified); how she feels about Bart's disappearance (although outwardly optimistic, especially in front of Kelley and Mitzi, inwardly she's terrified).

Together, Nathaniel and Scott are the perfect partner. Ava would like to live with them both forever or be married to each of them on alternating weeks. But since that practice isn't acceptable in Western cultures, Ava will have to choose, and she can't choose.

She needs time away with the wisest woman she knows.

*   *   *

Are there any woes that a five-star hotel in the Caribbean can't fix? The Malliouhana resort is set amid lush, impeccably manicured gardens that are silent but for the sound of a gurgling waterfall and birdsong. The spa is down one winding brick path, the fitness center down another. The lobby is Moroccan inspired, with marble floors and rattan ceiling fans and gracious arches that frame the expansive view of the turquoise sea. Ava is further charmed by their connecting suites—pencil-post beds with crisp linens and piles of fluffy white pillows, enormous soaking tubs, French champagne in the minibar, and a bright orange hammock chair on the balcony.

Who needs Nathaniel? Who needs Scott? Here, Ava has to decide only between her Jane Green novel and her Anita Shreve; between the hotel's infinity pool and one of three secluded beach coves; between rum punch and a glass of chilled rosé.

The first morning, Ava runs down the mile-long white crescent of sand that is Meads Bay, then, at the Viceroy hotel, she cuts in and runs another mile down the road. She passes a man, her age or a little older, who is wearing a Nantucket T-shirt and a hat from Cisco Brewers. Ava scowls—she can't get away! Nantucket is everywhere, even here on Anguilla! She gives the man a lame wave, then picks up her pace.

Margaret has gone to the fitness center and they meet for breakfast at ten o'clock in the open-air restaurant, both of them still in their workout clothes. At the buffet, Ava piles her plate with pineapple, papaya, and mango, whereas Margaret dives into the French cheeses, the ham, salami, and pâté, and the warm croissants. The woman can eat whatever she wants and never gain an ounce.

Ava sees the man in the Nantucket T-shirt sitting in the restaurant with a much-older gentleman, probably his father or his uncle or his boss. Margaret notices the Nantucket T-shirt and says to him, "Oh, my daughter lives on Nantucket!"

"No, Mom," Ava says, but it's too late, of course. The man whips off his hat and stands up.

He says, "You're Margaret Quinn."

Ava closes her eyes. She loves how her mother rolls through life like she's a normal person, seemingly unaware that every single soul in America—in the world, practically—recognizes her as the anchor of the *CBS Evening News*.

Margaret doesn't respond. Instead, she nudges Ava forward. "This is Ava," Margaret says. "She teaches music at the Nantucket Elementary School. Her father—my ex-husband—owns and operates the Winter Street Inn."

"Mom, he doesn't care," Ava says.

"No, I do care," the man says. "I'm Potter Lyons, and this is my grandfather, whose name is also Potter Lyons, but everyone calls him Gibby." Potter smiles at Ava. "I love Nantucket better than any place on earth. I go every August for Race Week. Do you sail?"

"We put her in sailing camp when she was seven years old," Margaret says. "There was a bully on her boat and she refused to go back. She hasn't sailed since." Margaret puts a thoughtful finger to her lips and turns to Ava. "Except that one summer when you sailed in the Opera House Cup."

Mom, he doesn't care! Ava thinks. He's only appearing interested because it's Margaret Quinn talking and she has a talent for making the mundane details of Ava's growing-up sound like national news.

Ava smiles at Potter and Gibby. "Confirmed," she says. "The bully's name was Alex, and in 2009, I sailed in the Opera House Cup on the *Shamrock*."

"They rent Sunfish here, down on the beach," Potter said. "It's not the *Shamrock,* but let me know if you want to go for a sail. I'd love to take you out."

Ava stares down at her plate of fruit. Her face is most likely the color of the papaya.

"Nice to meet you," she says. She leads her mother across the restaurant to the table farthest from Potter and Gibby.

"I think he likes you!" Margaret whispers.

No, Ava thinks. *He likes you.*

They bump into Potter and Gibby again at lunchtime at a place down the beach called Blanchards. Blanchards is a beach shack, and at first Ava is thrilled with the find. She and Margaret walk up to the counter in their bare feet and ask for one grilled mahimahi BLT with smoked-tomato tartar sauce, one order of shrimp tacos, and two sides of coleslaw. And while they're at it—two passion-fruit daiquiris.

Ava is so in love with the beach shack that she takes a picture of the menu and texts it to Kevin, saying, *You could do this at home! Quinns' on the Beach!* Kevin and Isabelle are running the inn, but Kevin has been looking for a second business opportunity. *This is it!* Ava thinks. Isabelle is a fantastic cook; she will be able to figure out the smoked-tomato tartar sauce, no problem.

Ava's reverie is interrupted by Potter and Gibby. "You've discovered our secret," Potter says. "We've eaten here six days straight."

"Jonum, phtzplz," Margaret says. Ava puts a hand on her mother's arm. The last thing Margaret needs is to be photographed with her mouth full of shrimp taco. She'll end up front and center in *Us Weekly*'s "Stars—They're Just Like Us!" (They talk with their mouths full!) Besides, Ava fears Margaret was trying to say *Join us, please.*

"We're almost done," Ava says, though she's taken only two bites of her heavenly sandwich.

"Hey, do you want to go for that sail later?" Potter asks.

Ava looks up at him. He's wearing orange board shorts and a white polo shirt. He has a little bit of gray in his dark hair, and his eyes seem very blue, probably thanks to his tan. He's way too handsome for her. He must be pursuing her because she's Margaret Quinn's daughter.

"Let me see how I feel later," she says.

The blue eyes light up. "Great!" he says.

When he and Gibby walk away, Margaret says, "You'd be a fool not to go."

"Mom," Ava says. "I have too many men in my life as it is."

"Sometimes what you need is a fresh perspective," Margaret says. "Go for a sail. It's not like you're marrying the guy."

Ava decides to ignore the fact that Potter is so good-looking and go for the sail. The first thing that happens is that the wind whips Potter's Cisco Brewers hat right off his head, and before either of them can react, it's dancing off toward the horizon.

"My favorite hat!" Potter says.

"Don't worry," Ava says. "I'll get you another one."

Potter Lyons is thirty-six years old. He's divorced and has a five-year-old son, also named Potter Lyons (though he goes by PJ), who lives with his mother in Palo Alto, California. Potter has a doctorate in American literature and teaches English at Columbia University. He wrote his dissertation on Jules Verne, *Twenty Thousand Leagues Under the Sea,* and he teaches the most popular class in the department, which is entitled the Nautical Novel: From the *Odyssey* to *Spartina.* He lives in a three-bedroom condo on the Upper West Side, only ten blocks north of Margaret, and he owns a sailboat, *Cassandra,* which he docks on the Hudson.

"Was Cassandra your wife?" Ava asks.

"My grandmother," he says.

Potter then tells her that his parents were killed in a car accident when he was in high school, and his grandparents—Gibby and Cassandra—took over raising him.

"My grandmother died a few months ago," Potter says. "So I planned this trip for Gibby. He needed to get away."

"I'm so sorry," Ava says.

"But enough about me," Potter says with a grin. "What do *you* think of me?"

Ava laughs. She thinks he's charming and smart, and she loves that he brought his grandfather on vacation.

"Just kidding," he says. "I want to hear about Ava."

"We'd have to sail to Cuba and back," she says.

He says, "I like complicated women. But just start by answering me this: Are you single?"

"No," she says. "I have two serious boyfriends." She is embarrassed by how absurd this sounds. "I love them both. I can't decide between them."

"Well, you know what that means," Potter says.

"What?"

He winks at her.

By the time Ava and Potter pull the boat back onto the shore, Ava has a fresh perspective: There are men everywhere—cute and smart and successful and available. Her choices aren't limited to Nathaniel and Scott.

She really likes Potter, for example.

"Do you want to meet for a drink later?" she asks.

"It's our last night," Potter says. "I think I'd better keep it just me and Gibby."

"Oh," Ava says. "All right." She feels a little...stung. How is this possible? She's been alone with this guy for only an hour. She wonders if she said something that turned him off. Possibly the thing about two serious boyfriends.

She hastens back to the infinity pool, where she finds Margaret lying on her chaise, eyes at half-mast. Ava is very proud of her mother. She works at her laptop for only an hour in the early morning, and she calls Drake every night before bed. Margaret is nothing if not disciplined, and on this trip she has been very disciplined about relaxing.

"How was the sail?" she asks. "Helpful?"

"Sort of," Ava says.

That night, Margaret and Ava wander down the beach to a place called Straw Hat, where all of the chandeliers are made of straw hats. It's the most charming thing Ava has ever seen, although she wonders when the hats will catch fire.

Ava drinks too much at dinner and starts to cry. "How did you know about Dad?" she asks Margaret. "How did you know he was the one you wanted to marry?"

"I was young and in love," Margaret says. "I didn't think about it. When he asked, of course I said yes. Kelley was amazing. He's still amazing. We wanted all the same things. We wanted careers in New York, we wanted a brownstone on the Upper East Side, we wanted three or four children. And guess what? We got everything we wanted, but we couldn't handle it. One of us had to give in, to concede, and that ended up being your father." Margaret takes a sip of wine. "A better question was how I decided about Drake, because I was very unsure for a long time. But then I realized that all marriages are a leap of faith. You love as hard as you can, you try to think of the other person first, and you hope for the best."

"What does it mean that I can't pick between them?" Ava says. "I like them both exactly the same amount, but for different reasons."

Margaret smiles. "I think it means you should keep your options open."

Ava and Margaret decide to have a nightcap at the bar at the hotel—and there, sitting alone, is Potter.

"Actually," Margaret says, "I should call Drake. He has an early surgery tomorrow."

"Then I'll head up to the room," Ava says. "I don't want to sit here by myself." But at that instant, Potter sees Ava and waves hello. Or maybe he's waving her over; Ava can't tell.

"I'll just say good night now," Margaret says. "I'll see you in the morning, sweetheart."

Ava watches her mother leave the bar and she nearly follows her out, but in another second, she's taking the stool next to Potter and ordering a glass of sauvignon blanc.

"Put that on my room," Potter says to the bartender. He smiles at Ava. "I was hoping I would see you here. Gibby went up to bed."

Ava's heart is a hummingbird.

Potter says, "What do you say we go for a walk on the beach? It's a beautiful night."

Ava sees no harm in a walk. There is a half-moon shining on the water, and the sound of piano music from another hotel floats down to the sand. They decide they'll walk to the Viceroy and back; that should be enough time for Ava to describe her dilemma. She tells Potter everything: how she had been dating Nathaniel for two years and he took her for granted, how he went away the Christmas before last and maybe slept with his old girlfriend or maybe didn't—Ava has never been brave enough to ask him—but while he was away, she hooked up with Scott, the assistant principal at the school where she teaches. She'd always known Scott liked her but she had never thought him sexy or desirable until... until he was nearly matched up with someone else. She dated Scott happily for a year while Nathaniel was conveniently away, working on Martha's Vineyard, and then, as luck would have it, Nathaniel returned to Nantucket on the very day that Scott went on this weird do-good mission with this other hot teacher who had broken her ankle. That was in December, Ava tells Potter, and since then, she has been dating both of them, openly. Her best friend, Shelby, thinks she's a wizard for living every woman's fantasy, but Ava is feeling torn in half every second of every day. She would like to feel whole.

"Wow," Potter says.

"I've talked too much," Ava says. They are nearly at the Viceroy; time to turn around. Potter is probably dying to get away.

"Not at all," Potter says. He reaches for her hand. Ava thinks maybe he hasn't been listening. She is torn between two other men... and yet Potter is now holding her hand. His hand is large and warm and strong—more like Scott's hand than Nathaniel's, although not really like Scott's hand at all—and holding it feels good. It feels like a fresh perspective.

"Why did you and your wife split?" Ava asks.

"We're both in academia," Potter says. "She's a Shakespeare scholar, which is not an uncrowded field, I'll tell you, and competition for spots is fierce. She got offered a tenure-track position at Stanford and I had the same at Columbia, but since I'd been working there longer, my salary was nearly double hers. At the time, PJ was two years old and couldn't be separated from Trish, so he went with her. We both sort of thought we might be able to make a bicoastal marriage work, but it didn't go that way. She fell in love with one of her teaching assistants."

"Oh," Ava says. "Ouch."

"He's British," Potter says. "She loves the accent."

They're almost back to the hotel but Ava doesn't want the walk to end. She says, "Look, there's our Sunfish!"

Potter says, "Would you like to sit for a minute?"

Potter kisses Ava as she sits on the bow of the Sunfish, just once, an exploratory mission, it seems, then they kiss again. And again.

Potter pulls away. "I'd love to see you the next time you come to the city," he says. "Or this summer on Nantucket. Can I give you my number?"

"Yes," Ava says. "And your address. I'm going to send you a new hat."

JENNIFER

She drives to exit 5 on Route 3 South, pulls into the parking lot of the Mayflower Deli, and waits. At a quarter after twelve, the black pickup drives up and parks beside her. Jennifer removes the envelope of cash from her purse and gets out of the car, scanning the lot for police or anyone who might be undercover. She casually walks to the driver's side. She hands Norah the envelope, and Norah hands Jennifer a Bayer aspirin bottle that contains fifty oxycodone pills.

Norah says, "When does Paddy get out?"

"June first," Jennifer says.

Norah's expression is sympathetic and Jennifer softens toward her former sister-in-law. Gone are the days when

Jennifer could claim some kind of moral superiority. Now, sadly, Norah is one of the most important people in Jennifer's life—her dealer. Jennifer had meant to quit the oxy after the holidays, but then she was faced with the quiet, cold weeks of January, and February brought Valentine's Day and her husband was *still* incarcerated. Then came March, with its surprisingly beautiful weather. Everyone in Boston had spring fever. The sidewalk cafés were packed; lovers held hands and lay on blankets on the Boston Common. Jennifer could see them from the window of her townhouse on Beacon Street. The sight depressed her. Then in April, Jennifer took the boys away for spring break—to San Francisco to visit her mother. There was no way she could handle a week with her mother without pharmaceutical help. So now she finds herself in May still buying drugs from Norah. Meanwhile, she's trying to parent three boys and run her interior design business. Today she has two large Kangxi blue-and-white porcelain vases, valued at over twenty-five grand apiece, in the back of her Volvo to deliver to a client in Duxbury.

"So will you be wanting any more, do you think?" Norah asks. Their implicit understanding has been that this new relationship of theirs will end once Patrick gets out of jail. Norah seems to be asking for confirmation of that. Does Norah possibly sense that Jennifer has become an addict? Well, yes, there is dependency, *obviously,* but is it permanent? Jennifer has blithely chosen to believe that once Patrick is back in the house, once he is back working, making money, helping out with the boys, and sleeping next to Jennifer in bed, there will be no need for the pills. Patrick's return will be her drug. Most likely, Norah is concerned only for her own welfare. Her lifestyle has certainly improved with this new line of work. Jennifer can hardly be her sole client; Norah is probably supplying pills to half the housewives between Mashpee and Mansfield. Her appearance has changed. She has started wearing Eileen Fisher in an eerie—or perhaps flattering?—echo of Jennifer herself. Norah Vale, once all denim and leather, is now silk and linen. And she's got on earrings that Jennifer recognizes as Jessica Hicks. Wow. At this rate, Jennifer might soon be *Norah's* decorator. The thought isn't all that outlandish.

Okay, Jennifer thinks, *time to leave.*

"I have to scoot," she says. "I have two Chinese vases waiting to meet their new parents."

"So this is it, then?" Norah says. She eyes the front of the deli. "You don't want to go in and grab a sandwich real quick, do you?"

Jennifer is touched, but also alarmed, mostly at her own feelings of fear and regret. She has grown to sort of like Norah now that their connection has nothing to do with the Quinn family, and she will miss their weekly meetings, in a way.

"I'll call you the next time I'm on the island," Jennifer says.

Norah's face falls. Both she and Jennifer know Jennifer will never call. Even if she wanted to, she couldn't.

"Okay, then," Norah says. "See you around."

KELLEY

The week after his final radiation treatment, Kelley returns to Mass. General for an MRI to determine if his cancer is gone. After a tense five-day wait, Dr. Cherith—a med-school classmate of Margaret's fiancé, Dr. Drake Carroll, as it turns out—calls to say Kelley appears to be in the clear.

"Cancer gone," Dr. Cherith says. "No guarantees, of course. But for now, safe to say you beat it."

After he hangs up, Kelley takes a deep yoga breath, then exhales in an *Om,* the way Mitzi has taught him. Gratitude to Mother Earth, gratitude to God above. He has beaten it. It wasn't easy; prostate cancer isn't glamorous. Kelley spent over a month in adult diapers, a fact he'd like to forget as soon as possible. And the radiation exhausted him. Thank God Mitzi had left George and come back to him. She took complete control of his treatment and made every decision. She brought Kelley breakfast in bed each morning—organic acai bowls with fruit and seeds and nuts—and every night, she read to him. They got through the first three Harry Potters, books Kelley had longed to read—he loved magical fantasy stories—but back when they were published, his kids were far too old for them and his grandchildren not old enough. Mitzi has a wonderful reading voice—clear and expressive— and at one point, Kelley had rolled toward her and said, "Have you ever considered a career in broadcasting?"

She glowered at him. "I'm Mitzi, Kelley. Not Margaret."

"I know that," Kelley had said, although he then realized he'd gotten mixed up for a second. That was another side effect of the radiation: mental confusion. Kelley had such intense dreams that he sometimes mistook them for reality. In the most vivid, the U.S. military made contact with members of the Afghan rebel group Bely, the faction that was holding Bart and his comrades prisoner, and asked what they would accept in exchange for the soldiers. The Bely had responded that they wanted Leonardo DiCaprio and a hundred dozen Mrs. Fields chocolate chip cookies. The transaction had gone through and Bart had come home, whole and unharmed, unmarred except for a tattoo of a star on his cheek. Mitzi had screamed—her baby's face!—but Kelley had simply gathered his son into his arms, kissed the star, and thought, *I am never letting this kid go.* When Kelley woke up, he'd experienced that particular elation one feels when something valuable that has been lost is returned. But then, upon realizing it was just a dream, Kelley fell back into his shallow pool of despair. William Burke, from Bart's platoon, is still unconscious. Back in February, he had been transported from Landstuhl in Germany to Walter Reed in Bethesda and the whole world is waiting for his condition to improve. Kelley had toyed with the idea of going to Bethesda himself to visit William Burke—Kelley had just enough hubris to believe that his presence might be the very thing to snatch Private Burke from the jaws of darkness. But Mitzi told Kelley the idea was impractical. He had to fight his own battle.

He has fought the battle and emerged victorious!

He will tell everyone the news soon enough. But first, Kelley is going to walk down Main Street to the Nantucket Pharmacy lunch counter, where he will order the ham-and-pickle sandwich on rye bread and a chocolate frappe. He has been dreaming of this exact lunch for months, but it has remained a fantasy. While he was sick, Mitzi put him on an organic vegetarian diet.

If Kelley never sees a leaf of kale again, it will be too soon.

KEVIN

After breakfast most days, Kevin takes his daughter, Genevieve, to Children's Beach and pushes her on the baby swing. It's his favorite hour of the day. As soon as he releases Genevieve from the straps of the stroller, she starts kicking her legs and making hoots of anticipation. Then, once she's buckled into the swing and Kevin pushes her, she starts to belly-laugh. The other parents at Children's Beach are all mothers and they comment on what a gorgeous baby Genevieve is and what a devoted father Kevin seems to be. On the one hand, this makes Kevin feel like a superstar—the mothers anticipate his arrival at the park and compete for his attention—but on the other, it makes him feel like a loser. He's here at the park with the *mothers*. Their husbands are at work. Kevin, too, should be at work.

For over a year, Kevin and Isabelle have been running the Winter Street Inn. Kevin assumed Mitzi's duties when Mitzi left, and then when Kelley got sick, he took over Kelley's duties as well. But two weeks earlier, Kelley was given a clean bill of health. He and Mitzi are back together and, suddenly, there are three jobs for four people. Isabelle is indispensable—she is the cook and the housekeeping manager. All Kevin has proved useful for is taking the heavy loads of dirty linen down to the basement.

Kevin needs another job. He toys with going back to the Bar, but the day shift doesn't bring in any tips, and if he works at night, he'll never see Isabelle. A few weeks earlier, Margaret and Ava went to Anguilla on vacation and Ava texted Kevin a photo of a beach shack where they ate lunch every day. She said: *You could do this at home! Quinns' on the Beach!* Kevin had studied the menu. Grilled-fish sandwiches, tacos, rice bowls, flatbreads, salads, frozen drinks, ice cream. Ava's right; Nantucket needs a place like this. There is the Jetties on the north shore—and what a gold mine that place has turned out to be—but the south shore, which is where all the teenagers and college kids hang out, is a lunch wasteland. The shack on Surfside Beach used to sell hamburgers, hot dogs, and ice pops but it shut down a few years ago. Could Kevin take over the lease and turn it into something better than it had ever been?

It wouldn't hurt to find out.

His thoughts of striped-bass BLTs are interrupted by Haven Silva, a girl Kevin went to high school with and who is now one of the Children's Beach mommies. Haven has gained a lot of clout with the other mothers because she knows Kevin from another life. The two of them are in a private club, of sorts; they both grew up on the island. Haven really grew up here—was born and raised—as opposed to Kevin, who summered on Nantucket from infancy to age fourteen, when he moved here year-round. Kevin marvels at how his fellow islanders feel like family to him. He remembers Haven with braces; he remembers that she left for boarding school at Tabor in their sophomore year but was back by Christmas because her younger brother, Danny, had had a seizure during recess and died. Kevin had gone to the funeral; the whole island had gone to the funeral. After college, Haven returned to Nantucket. She waitressed at the Lobster Trap for a while, then took the office-manager position at Don Allen Ford. Her mother died, and Haven moved back in with her father—and in this way, Haven and Kevin were in similar boats. But in recent years, they agreed, the gods have smiled upon them. Haven married a mechanic and had a little boy she named Daniel, after her brother. Kevin got together with Isabelle and had Genevieve.

"Kev," Haven says. "Do you have a second?"

"What's up?" Kevin says.

Haven positions herself just behind Kevin's right ear, out of the way of the trajectory of Genevieve's swing. Kevin does a daddy-scan of the playground. He sees the other mothers—Deborah, Rebecca, Wendy—sneaking glances at him and Haven. Haven's son, Daniel, is in the sandbox playing with his front-end loader.

"I heard a rumor about someone you know," Haven says. "And I think it's legit. Something Norm heard at the shop."

Kevin is, admittedly, a part of this little mom clique but he draws the line at gossiping with them. He doesn't want to hear any rumors. However, his immediate next thought is: *What could it be?* In general, the Quinn family has combated rumors by just coming out and telling the truth. Yes, Patrick went to jail for insider trading. Yes, Bart has been taken prisoner in Afghanistan. Yes, Mitzi left their father for George the Santa Claus. Yes, Ava is dating both Nathaniel Oscar and Scott Skyler. Yes, Kelley has prostate cancer. Yes, Mitzi came back to Kelley. Yes, Kelley's cancer is in remission. What else is there? Kevin wonders if the rumor is about Isabelle. She has never once brought Genevieve to the park. He realizes the other mothers wonder about this.

"Do I even want to know?" Kevin says.

Haven twists her mouth. "Probably not. I've sat on this a couple days already. If you don't want to hear, tell me to go away."

"What is it?" Kevin says. He pushes Genevieve and she coos with delight. Nothing Haven Silva tells him can ruin this moment.

"It's about Norah Vale," Haven says.

"Oh, come on," Kevin says. Norah Vale is Kevin's ex-wife, the person he cares about least in the world. He wouldn't give her a second's attention except that Norah has moved back to Nantucket for a seemingly indefinite period, so every time Kevin leaves the house—to go to the grocery store or the gas station—it's like a game of dodgeball. He can't bump into her, even accidentally. Isabelle will kill him. Every so often, Kevin will see Norah's black pickup on the road, but he keeps his eyes straight ahead. He won't bother to lift two fingers from the steering wheel in greeting.

"I guess she's got quite a drug-dealing operation going," Haven says. "Pharmaceuticals."

Kevin shakes his head. "That's so unsurprising, I can't believe it even counts as gossip."

"She has a bunch of high-end clients," Haven says. "Apparently the ladies-who-summer are washing Vicodins down with those bottles of rosé when they have lunch at the Galley."

"Good for Norah," Kevin says. He doesn't even like saying her name out loud. "She found a niche market."

"The story gets worse," Haven says.

Kevin closes his eyes.

"I guess. And this is only what I *heard,* Kev..."

"What?" he says impatiently. He can guarantee he doesn't want to hear the next sentence out of Haven Silva's mouth.

"One of her clients is your sister-in-law."

"My..." It takes Kevin a second. His sister-in-law? Which sister-in-law? No, wait, there is only one: Jennifer. "Jennifer? Patrick's wife, Jennifer?"

"That's what I heard," Haven says. "I thought you'd want to know."

Kevin finds Haven's tone so irritating that his first instinct is to tell her that she's part of the problem. Probably she has shared this juicy nugget with all of the other mothers here at Children's Beach. Norah Vale, his ex-wife, is purportedly selling pills to his sister-in-law, Jennifer. Jennifer hates Norah. Even when they were part of the same family, Jennifer didn't have a nice word for Norah. And vice versa.

But Kevin applies his verbal brakes. He can't lose his temper with Haven Silva. First of all, she's telling him only because he should know the rumor is out there. Second, and far more important, Haven's uncle Chester Silva is one of Nantucket's five selectmen, and if Kevin wants to lease the Surfside shack, he's going to need Chester's support.

Kevin smiles at Haven and the smile is sincere. She named her son after her beloved younger brother, taken from them too soon. She is a good person.

"I doubt it's true," Kevin says. He lifts Genevieve out of the swing and she squawks in protest. "But thank you for letting me know."

SUMMER

JENNIFER

Patrick's release from jail is delayed by three weeks.

Why? Why? Jennifer wants to know why.

"I'm not sure why," Patrick says over the phone. "Maybe I understood it wrong to begin with? Janine in Processing was adamant. I get out the twenty-first, not the first."

Patrick sounds like he's just going to roll over and accept his fate rather than fight it. He has been in jail too long; he's become submissive. Where is her take-charge, fix-everything husband?

"Have you called Hollis?" Jennifer asks.

"I called him, he knows, but there's nothing he can do about it, and even if there were something he could do about it, it would likely take the same amount of time I have to wait anyway. It's only three more weeks," Patrick says. "I've gotten through eighteen months. I can wait three more weeks."

Maybe he can, but Jennifer can't. June 1 is decorated with a pink heart on her calendar. In her mind, the day is a starburst. She has rationed her energy and her patience to make it to June 1—not a day longer. And certainly not three weeks longer. She has already planned a family dinner for Patrick's first night home—poached salmon with mustard-dill sauce and the crispy potato croquettes that Patrick loves. And then the following two nights, Jennifer has farmed the boys out on sleepovers so that she and Patrick can have the house to themselves. She has bought new lingerie and new sheets; she has ordered a tin of osetra caviar and chilled a vintage bottle of Veuve. She has told Jaime, their youngest, that Patrick will make it to his final lacrosse game of the season. The plans are so embedded in Jennifer's mind that she can't shift them forward three weeks. She just can't!

"It sounds like you *want* to stay in jail," Jennifer says. "Maybe you have a little romance going on with Janine from Processing."

"Jennifer," Patrick says. "Please."

"Please *what?*"

"Please try to understand. This isn't my fault. It isn't anyone's fault. It was a misunderstanding. A scheduling glitch."

Jennifer nods into the phone but she can't speak. She knows it's not Patrick's fault. She knows she should accept this news gracefully and adjust her expectations. She's an interior designer. She, of all people, understands delays. It happens all the time in her business—carpets from India get stuck in Customs, quarries run out of a particular kind of granite, her son Barrett gets walking pneumonia and Jennifer has to postpone an installation by a week.

"Okay," she says. "We'll see you on the twenty-first."

"That's my girl," Patrick says.

Jennifer hangs up the phone. Immediately, she calls Norah Vale.

It's June 20, the first day of summer, when Jennifer drives out to Shirley, Massachusetts, to pick Patrick up. She can't seem to control her nerves, despite eating two Ativan for breakfast. Her heart is slamming in her chest, almost as if she's afraid. Afraid of what? She went to visit Patrick a week ago Thursday and talked to him yesterday afternoon, but this is different. He's coming home. He's coming home!

Patrick is standing by the gate with his favorite guard, Becker, a man even Jennifer has come to know and appreciate. Jennifer barely remembers to put the car in park. She jumps out and runs into Patrick's arms. He picks her up and they kiss like crazy teenagers until Becker clears his throat and says, "You all need to get a room."

Patrick shakes Becker's hand and says, "Thanks for having my back, man. I'm gonna miss you."

"No, you won't," Becker says with a smile. "Now get out of here."

Patrick drives them home. He says, "It's like the world is brand-new. I missed driving."

"You hate driving," Jennifer says.

"I'll never complain about it again," Patrick says. "I'll never complain about anything again."

It's a good lesson about the things we take for granted, Jennifer thinks. Patrick reenters the free world with the enthusiasm of a child.

Jennifer says, "What do you want to do first?"

He gives her a look as if to say *Do you even have to ask that?*

She swats his arm. "After that."

"I want to hug my children," he says.

"Obviously," Jennifer says. "After that."

"I want to stop at the store and get a cold six-pack," he says. "I want to smell a flower. I want to take a bath. I want to get into a bed with my head on three fluffy pillows. I want to swim in the ocean. I want to go to the movies and get popcorn with too much butter. I want a glass of water filled with ice. You have no idea how much I've missed ice. I want to walk across Boston Common and smell the marijuana smoke and get asked for spare change. I want to wear my watch. I want to download music. I want to watch the sun go down. I want to throw the lacrosse ball with Jaime. I want to meet my new niece. I want my electric toothbrush. I want to wear *my* shirts, *my* boxers, *my* loafers." He pauses. He seems overcome. "There are so many things."

"There will be time," Jennifer says. "I promise." She knows what he means. He's here, right here next to her. She puts her hand on the back of his head. She never wants to stop touching him.

"And you," Patrick says. "You are amazing. You held everything together. You were *so* strong. You deserve a medal. I wouldn't have blamed you if you'd left me, Jenny."

"I would never leave you," she says.

"I don't know how you did it," he says. "I don't know how you got through the days. It must have been so hard on you and yet you never complained. You are my hero, Jennifer Barrett Quinn."

She longs to confess: *I'm addicted to pills. Completely, pathetically addicted.*

But instead she says, "Stop. You're embarrassing me."

AVA

June 20 is the first day of summer and the last day of school. Ava can remember only one other year when the two converged, but everyone finds it fitting: a seasonal passing of the baton.

The day is sweltering, and naturally, tradition dictates that the majority of the last day be spent with the entire school packed together in the gymnasium, the one room in the building that defies even the most powerful air-conditioning. Ava has begged Principal Kubisch to keep the two back doors propped open for ventilation, despite the fact that, in this day and age, it's a security violation.

There is a pint-size version of pomp and circumstance for the departing fifth-graders, and Ava is overcome with nostalgia. She remembers Ryan Papsycki and Topher Fotea and the clique now headed by Sophie Fairbairn back when they were tiny kindergartners. Today, Sophie has seen fit to wear a lace bustier and show off her double-pierced ears. She'll be a big hit in middle school.

Ava herds the fourth-graders into rows of chairs for their three minutes of fame. They have been practicing "Annie's Song," by John Denver, on their recorders ever since they got back from Christmas break and they've gotten proficient enough that Ava doesn't have to put in earplugs when they play it. She and Scott have an ongoing debate about how teaching the recorder should have been banned back in 1974 after the first class of students learned to play "Annie's Song." The recorder is such a lame instrument! Ava would far prefer teaching something the kids might actually use later in life—the harmonica, say, or the ukulele, the xylophone or the bongo drums. Anything but the recorder.

Ava raises her arms and imagines for a moment that she is Arthur Fiedler conducting the Boston Pops. Ha! That's funny enough that Ava nearly breaks into a grin. D'laney Rodenbough still has her recorder swaddled in a striped kneesock, but Ava can't wait for D'laney. It's too hot and everyone wants to get out of there.

You fill up my senses . . .

The song is over in two minutes and thirty-six seconds and as Ava zips her hands over her head, like she's closing up the school year and all the laughter, learning, rule-breaking, and scolding that went with it, she sees, standing by the open back door, the tall, authoritative figure of the assistant principal, Scott Skyler, and, next to him, Roxanne Oliveria.

The assembled crowd applauds. Ava takes a shallow bow. The person inside Ava shakes her head in disgust. What is Mz. Ohhhhhh doing here?

Ava's best friend, Shelby, the school librarian, grabs Ava's arm as they're walking out of the gym. "She's shameless."

"I'm sure he invited her," Ava says.

"Only to make you jealous," Shelby says.

Ava thinks that this is probably true.

Somehow, Scott and Mz. Ohhhhhh have teleported themselves from the back door of the gym to just outside the main office, where they are jointly waving good-bye to the students, like Mr. and Mrs. America on a parade float. Ava is so perplexed—what is Roxanne *doing* here?—that she allows herself to be carried along on a wave of students giddy with escape.

She gets close enough that Roxanne can grab Ava's arm. "Congratulations!" she says.

"Thanks?" Ava says.

"This is my favorite day of the year," Roxanne says.

Ava makes a face. Roxanne teaches high school English. The high school got out last week. For the past seven days, Roxanne has been reading the new Nancy Thayer novel and catching up on Netflix.

Whatever, Ava thinks. She wants to get away, but there are kids everywhere. Scott is involved in high-fiving all of the children from his special advisory group, kids who were considered "at risk" at the beginning of the year but who are now contributing citizens.

"...Tuscany?" Roxanne says.

Ava looks at her, alarmed. Is Roxanne still talking to her?

"I'm sorry?" Ava says.

"Did Scott tell you he's taking me to Tuscany?" Roxanne says. "We've rented a villa."

Ava is too blindsided to bluff. "No," she says. "He did not tell me that."

"We leave tonight," Roxanne says.

Ava collects her things from her room. The previous year on the last day of school, she and Scott had stopped at Henry's Jr. for sandwiches and Hatch's for beer and then had driven Ava's Jeep up to Great Point, where they stayed until the sun went down.

Tuscany. A villa.

Ava had had drinks with Scott on Saturday night at the Jetties. Drinks turned into a dozen oysters at the bar, which turned into dinner. Marshall sat them at the table he called Romance No. 1, set apart from all the other tables and lit only by candles. They ordered a crisp white wine and the lobster pizza and they listened to the guitar player do a pretty creative acoustic version of "Paradise by the Dashboard Light." Ava went back to Scott's place afterward and then in the morning, they'd gone to the Downyflake for breakfast, where they saw half the school faculty. Ava told Scott how excited she was to work with Kevin at Quinns' on the Beach—four days a week, eleven to five.

Scott had kissed Ava and said, "But I'll never see you."

"You can come visit," Ava said. "I'll make you a frappe."

Scott had not said word one about taking Roxanne to Tuscany or renting a villa.

Ava bristles. Scott has never taken Ava anywhere except to Tuckernuck, which is a whopping half a mile from Madaket Harbor by boat. They had stayed two nights in the old schoolhouse, which was appropriate for two educators. The schoolhouse was home to field mice and spiders, and Ava had to relieve herself in a bucket. It was not a villa in Tuscany.

She considers sending Scott a text—but what would she say? That she's hurt? Obviously, he realizes this. That he should have told Ava himself instead of letting Roxanne drop the news like a dirty bomb? Obviously, he realizes this as well. Next, Ava considers sending Shelby a text, but Shelby has a husband and a cute baby boy waiting for her at home. She claims she loves hearing about the drama in Ava's life, but she's lying.

Ava slogs through the heat out to the parking lot. Silence will be her weapon of choice, she decides. Scott can go to Tuscany tomorrow, he can have fun dancing Roxanne around their villa to "Brown-Eyed Girl," Ava doesn't care. She won't call, she won't text. She will be a stone wall of impenetrable silence, a fortress of noncommunication.

Then Ava finds a dozen pale pink roses lying across the front seat of her Jeep. Her heart lifts briefly—Scott? There's a note on top: *Congrats, babe! Meet me on the Straight Wharf tonight at 7:30 sharp. Love, N.*

Nathaniel.

Ava can't help herself; she feels let down. She wonders if this means she's any closer to solving her quandary. Does she really love Scott? Or is it a false construct—she loves Scott only because Scott is taking Roxanne to Tuscany?

She lifts the roses and inhales. She stands in the parking lot sniffing her lavish bouquet a little longer than she might have normally, hoping that Scott will come out and see her.

His Explorer is three cars away from her car in the parking lot. Has Scott ever expressed *any* interest in going to Italy? Africa, yes, the Peace Corps—a lifelong dream. But Italy? Scott doesn't even like Italian food!

After another few seconds, Ava feels like an idiot. She tosses the roses onto the passenger seat and drives home to the inn.

At home, there is a bottle of Veuve Clicquot sitting on ice on the kitchen counter.

For me? she wonders. That doesn't seem right. Ava's family is wonderful and nurturing, but would anyone have remembered that it was her last day of school and chosen to celebrate it?

Mitzi and Kelley are both in the kitchen. Mitzi is reaching for the champagne flutes and Kelley is pulling the blueberry Brie out of the oven. Kelley never serves his blueberry Brie to the guests; it's strictly a family treat. But what's the occasion?

"Hey," Ava says, "I'm home."

"Just in time," Kelley says. He sets the Brie on the counter and Ava gazes at it longingly.

"What's going on?" she asks, and then her eyes bulge. Have they found Bart?

"Your brother," Kelley says.

Ava starts to shake. Her chest constricts. She has imagined Bart's return every day since he went missing. She's imagined the instant she hears the news; she's imagined her wondrous relief, the anxiety being lifted off her shoulders by a host of angels. But no, no, she thinks—Mitzi isn't emotional enough. If it were Bart, Mitzi would be on her knees, weeping.

"My brother?" Ava says.

"Patrick," Kelley says. "He got out of jail this morning."

"Right," Ava says. In a side pocket of her mind, she'd known this. "Is he here?"

"No," Mitzi says. "He's at home with Jennifer and the kids. But we decided to celebrate anyway."

Ava nods and accepts a champagne flute. She feels a twinge of irritation. They're celebrating the brother who broke the law and ended up in jail while the brother who set out to defend the country's freedom is—best-case scenario—imprisoned by enemy forces. But...okay? They're the Quinns! Ava supposes she should just drink her champagne, eat the most delicious cheese on earth, and celebrate Patrick's release.

Kevin, Isabelle, and Genevieve stroll into the kitchen. Kevin swings Genevieve between his legs.

"You're going to dislocate her shoulders!" Mitzi cries.

"She's tough," Kevin says, then he lifts her up and kisses her cheek. "My tough baby girl."

The time with her family does wonders for Ava's mood. After a glass and a half of champagne and two crostini smothered with the gooey, fruity cheese, Ava repairs to the shower. She'll meet Nathaniel on the Straight Wharf, and she will wear a knockout dress and put her hair in a loose bun the way he likes it.

"Are you going out with Scott or Nathaniel tonight?" Mitzi asks as Ava heads out the back door of the inn.

"Nathaniel," Ava says. "Scott is going to Tuscany with Roxanne."

"Oh," Mitzi says. "Oh my."

Nathaniel is standing at the start of the Straight Wharf, just in front of the Gazebo. He's holding a bottle of Veuve Clicquot and two champagne flutes.

This time Ava feels certain the champagne is for her.

"Where are we going?" she asks.

"Follow me," he says.

He leads her down the dock to where the fishing boats are lined up and stops at the *Endeavor*. The *Endeavor* is a thirty-one-foot Friendship sloop that does charter harbor cruises, specializing in sunsets; Kelley and Mitzi recommend it for guests of the inn all the time. Ava loves seeing the boat on the horizon; she always imagines how lucky the people on board are. She hasn't been on the boat since Mitzi rented it for Kelley's fiftieth birthday.

"Are we going?" she asks Nathaniel.

"We're going," he says.

"By ourselves?"

"Just you and me, the captain, and the first mate."

Ava can't believe it. This is an extravagant gesture. In her mind, it's even better than a villa in Tuscany. Ava removes her shoes and climbs aboard with Nathaniel following. The hot day has turned into a mild evening, and because it's the longest day of the year, there's still an hour of daylight before sunset. Ava stretches out on the bow—they're the only guests; they have the whole boat to themselves!—and Nathaniel joins her. He pops the cork on the champagne and pours two glasses. They putter out of the slip and into the harbor.

Ava has lived on Nantucket since she was nine years old, but she is still dazzled every time she gets out on the water. It doesn't happen as often as one might think. She takes the ferry, of course, and on the occasional summer Sunday, she will join Shelby and Zack in their whaler for a trip to Coatue or Great Point. But given that Ava's usually at school or the inn, most of her Nantucket experience takes place on land.

The sails go up as the boat rounds Brant Point Light.

There are a couple of kids on the beach collecting horseshoe crabs. Ava waves at them. The *Endeavor* sails around the jetty and out into Nantucket Sound. Ava sees the Cliffside Beach Club and the Galley restaurant. Piano music and the clink of glasses drift over the water. The sun lowers on the horizon, a ball of pink fire.

Nathaniel is wearing a white linen shirt and the faded madras shorts that are her favorite. Nathaniel's a builder and works outside, so he's already very tan, and he's let the scruff on his face grow for three days. Ava loves it this way.

He is so handsome, she thinks. *And talented and funny. He can have any girl he wants.* She looks at the water.

"This is..." Ava says. She's worried that by choosing a word, any word, she will be limiting the magnificence and beauty of the night. "It's..."

"Ava," Nathaniel says.

She turns. He's holding a black box.

He opens the box. Diamond ring.

"I want you to be my wife," he says. "Will you marry me?"

Ava blinks. She looks at the ring sparkle; she looks into Nathaniel's green eyes, notices the slightly nervous set of his smile, and then casts her gaze up. Across the darkening sky are the contrails of an airplane. Ava imagines it's Scott and Roxanne's plane, heading to Tuscany.

"Yes," she says.

Nathaniel stands up on the bow and raises his arms in a V. "She said yes!" he shouts. "She! Said! Yes!"

Ava laughs. She gets to her feet and kisses him.

From behind the wheel, the captain calls out, "Congratulations!"

"Thank you!" Ava says. Her eyes follow the trajectory of the contrails until they fade away.

*   *   *

Later, over a dinner of oyster sliders and lobster rolls at Cru, Nathaniel says, "I signed on for a new job today."

"Yeah," Ava says. "As Mr. Ava Quinn." She can't stop looking at the ring on her finger. She feels like a completely different person—a person who has been proposed to, and in the most romantic way possible.

"Well, yeah," Nathaniel says. "And I also got a new building job. It's a compound like nothing I've ever seen—a six-thousand-square-foot main house, a pool house, a four-car garage, and three guest cottages for the kids."

"Wow," Ava says. She greatly respects Nathaniel's skills as a carpenter—he is held in very high esteem professionally—but where work is concerned, she has more in common with Scott.

She has to stop comparing them, she thinks. She's made her decision, right? Nathaniel. She looks at the ring. She hates herself for imagining what Scott will do when she tells him, but the shocked, incredulous expression that will appear on his face keeps looping through her mind. *Please don't tell me you only said yes to Nathaniel in order to one-up the trip to Tuscany,* she scolds herself.

"Where is it?" Ava asks. "The job?"

She's expecting him to say Shimmo or Madaket, Quaise or Madequecham. Or, maybe . . . Sconset. (Like a true islander, she thinks: *Please not Sconset. It's so far away!*)

"Block Island," he says.

She gapes. Her jaw drops, her eyes pop, her mind races. *Block Island?*

Last year, Nathaniel did an enormous project on Martha's Vineyard. Chappaquiddick, to be specific. At least Ava has reference points for the Vineyard—it's got seven towns to Nantucket's one and it's fifteen miles closer to the mainland.

Ava has been to the Vineyard at least a dozen times. She has shopped at Nell's in Edgartown, jogged down the bike path to Katama Bay, seen the requisite sunset from the bluffs of Aquinnah, and eaten ice cream at Mad Martha's. But the only thing she knows about Block Island is that it's part of Rhode Island.

"I'd like to get married before we move there," Nathaniel says.

"We?" Ava says.

"Yes," Nathaniel says. "We."

Ava gulps and slides the ring off her finger.

KELLEY

Kelley and Mitzi are hosting Margaret and Drake's wedding on August 20. Margaret calls the inn, and both Kelley and Mitzi get on the phone to discuss the details. Margaret wants to keep it *simple, simple, simple.* Just family and a few close friends, she says—but where to draw the line? Margaret and Drake; Kelley and Mitzi; Patrick, Jennifer, and the kids; Kevin, Isabelle, and Genevieve; Ava and Scott; Margaret's assistant, Darcy; Drake's nephew, Liam; Ava's friends Shelby and Zack; Jennifer's mother, Beverly, from San Francisco; Drake's colleague Jim Hahn and his wife, but not their five children. Margaret has to invite Lee Kramer, the head of the network, and his wife, Ginny, who is the editor of *Vogue,* but Margaret is pretty sure they'll decline. They're Hamptons people.

Mitzi says, "Would it be too off-the-wall to invite George and Mary Rose?"

"Yes," Kelley says.

"If you want to invite George, it's fine with me," Margaret says. "He has been a part of our larger story this past year."

You can say that again! Kelley thinks. He knows that Mitzi and George Umbrau—the man Mitzi had been conducting an affair with for twelve straight Christmases when he came to the Winter Street Inn to play Santa Claus—parted on good terms. He also knows that George is now hot and heavy with Mary Rose Garth, a woman he met here on Nantucket last Stroll weekend during the Holiday House Tour. Who knew George was such a player? Kelley doesn't feel threatened by George, not really; the attraction between him and Mitzi has run its course. And Mitzi is being very gracious in hosting Kelley's ex-wife's wedding.

"Sure, let's invite George and Mary Rose," Kelley says. George is fun at parties. And Kelley would basically do anything to keep Mitzi's mind off Bart.

A few days earlier, Walter Reed National Military Medical Center finally issued a press release about the status of Private William Burke. The soldier had regained consciousness but was still unable to speak. He could answer simple questions by blinking his eyes. Kelley and Mitzi had hugged each other in celebration, although they soon realized they weren't any closer to getting answers about Bart.

What kind of simple questions are the doctors asking the private? Kelley wonders. Is he alert enough to answer questions about what happened? About his fellow troops, still held captive? And what if . . .

The next thought is too difficult to articulate, even in his mind. What if William Burke says that he's the sole survivor? What if William Burke's regaining consciousness is the end of hope?

Again, Kelley considers driving ten hours south to Bethesda—but that won't solve anything. He and Mitzi simply have to wait. They have to live their lives and concentrate on the family they do have.

Margaret and Drake's wedding will be held on the beach out at Eel Point. Catherine, the town clerk, will marry Margaret and Drake, and there will be a harp player, a trumpet player, and a cellist. But Margaret keeps adding surprises. At the beginning of August, Margaret and Drake had dinner at the Club Car. When they visited the piano bar in the back, Margaret met Gordon Russell, a man with a deep, resonant, nearly professional-sounding singing voice. He had been belting out "Oh, What a Beautiful Mornin'" from *Oklahoma!* Margaret (a lifelong sucker for show tunes) approached Mr. Russell afterward and asked him to sing at her wedding. And, because Margaret is an investigative reporter, she learned that Mr. Russell owned the Lilly Pulitzer store In the Pink, here on Nantucket, and that he was a twelfth-generation islander, descended from the Folgers and the Gardners. In all ways, Gordon Russell is a valuable, interesting addition to the group.

"What song is he singing?" Kelley asks.

" 'The Wedding Song,' " Margaret says casually.

This gives Kelley pause. "The Wedding Song"? The old chestnut sung by Paul Stookey of Peter, Paul, and Mary that was so in vogue forty years earlier when Margaret and Kelley got married? Hadn't he and Margaret wanted Kelley's brother, Avery, to sing "The Wedding Song" at *their* wedding? Yes, Kelley is pretty sure they had, but then the priest wouldn't allow it, so one of the choir members had sung the Ave Maria instead.

"But that was our song," Kelley says.

"It wasn't our song," Margaret says. "Our song was 'Thunder Road.' 'The Wedding Song' was only a song we considered for the ceremony. Don't be sensitive."

Is Kelley being sensitive? Probably. What does it matter if Margaret is recycling their first choice of song? This wedding requires adult behavior from everyone.

After all, Kelley will be giving Margaret away.

KEVIN

Quinns' on the Beach is a gangbuster success, a beyond-his-wildest-dreams moneymaking machine. Kevin hasn't slept since Memorial Day, but by the end of Fourth of July weekend, he is able to pay Kelley and Margaret back the money they lent him to get the business up and running. From the time the shack opens, at eleven o'clock in the morning, until it closes, at five, there is a line all the way through the parking lot to the road. Quinns' on the Beach is written up in *N Magazine,* the blog *Mahon About Town,* and the *Inquirer and Mirror.* People are crazy about the striped-bass BLT made with Bartlett's Farm tomatoes, gem lettuce, and lemon-herb mayonnaise and presented on a soft pumpernickel roll. On an average day, he sells two hundred sandwiches at fifteen bucks apiece.

If Kevin weren't so bone-tired, he would be ecstatically happy. Finally, finally, *finally,* at the age of thirty-eight he has done it: found his calling. He is no longer slinging drinks at the Bar. He is no longer working for his father. By the end of the season—he'll stay open seven days a week through Labor Day, then on weekends only until Columbus Day—he reckons he'll have enough money that he, Isabelle, and Genevieve can find their own place to live.

There are many things Kevin loves about Quinns' other than the money. For example, he loves working with Ava. He figures that could have gone either way, but the two of them have turned out to be an outstanding team. Ava is brilliant at taking orders and manning the register. He loves to hear her banter with the kids, especially her students from the elementary school. She also excels at the upsell—lobster tacos instead of beef tacos, frappes instead of sodas. And she has phenomenal taste in music. For the shack, she made a variety of playlists. There's the Tropical playlist (Buffett, Bob Marley, Michael Franti), the Classic Rock playlist (Stones, Clapton, Zeppelin), and the Acoustic playlist (Coldplay, James Taylor, some long-lost Springsteen tracks).

Kevin sees every person he has ever known, and he meets new people every day. During the week, it's mostly moms and kids, teenagers, and college students, but on the weekends, the fathers show up.

"I really wish you sold beer," they all say.

"Me too," Kevin says. "Next year." As soon as the place closes for the season, he'll figure out whose ass he has to kiss to get a liquor license.

Isabelle brings Genevieve every day at four thirty, and Ava takes the baby while Isabelle finishes with the customers and tallies the day's receipts. Isabelle isn't as good with people as Ava is but it's important for Isabelle to get the exposure and practice her English.

One day, Haven Silva comes through the line with her son, Daniel. Kevin flashes back to their conversation that spring about Norah selling pills to Jennifer and he hopes and prays she doesn't bring it up. If she were to mention it to Ava, Ava would have a cow. She would call Patrick and Jennifer as soon as she got home and demand answers. That's because Ava likes to deal with problems head-on, whereas Kevin prefers to bury them in his mind at the bottom of the pile known as Quinn Family Dirty Laundry.

Haven orders lobster tacos, a kid's bacon burger, and two frappes. She grins at Kevin and gives him an enthusiastic thumbs-up. "I'm happy for you!"

Phew, he thinks.

But then, sometime during the insanity that is the second week of August—when all the residents of the Eastern Seaboard have crammed themselves onto Nantucket—the inevitable happens: Norah Vale comes through the line. Ava has run to the ladies' room, so Kevin is a sitting duck.

"Hey, Kev," Norah says.

The line behind Norah is two thousand people long. Kevin doesn't have time for any kind of scene or breakdown. If it were legal, he would have a sign on the front of the building reading OPEN TO THE PUBLIC (*except Norah Vale*).

"What can I get you?" he asks.

Norah scans the menu behind his head but it feels to Kevin like she's trying to read his mind.

"You got your own place," she says. "Proud of you."

"Thanks," he says. "What can I get you?"

"I'll have the fish BLT," she says. "Extra mayo. Side of coleslaw. And a coffee frappe. Please."

Kevin scribbles the order down. Where is Ava? He's so flustered by Norah's presence that he can barely do the math. It's only two fifteen, which is right in the middle of Genevieve's nap time, so there's no chance Isabelle will show up and see Kevin talking to Norah. But still.

"How's your family?" Norah asks.

"That'll be twenty-one dollars and sixty cents," Kevin says.

Norah pulls out her wallet and makes a show of flipping

through a wad of cash. Hundreds and hundreds of dollars, it seems. So the drug-dealing part is probably true.

"Hey, Kev, I'll take over here." Ava is back, thank God! She squeezes his arm. "Hello, Norah."

"Ava," Norah says. "I was just asking after your family. Everyone good?"

"Good," Ava confirms. She takes twenty-five dollars from Norah and gives her change, which Norah stuffs into the tip jar.

"That'll be eight to ten minutes," Ava says.

"How's Jennifer?" Norah asks.

Kevin freezes.

"Jennifer?" Ava says.

"Norah," Kevin says. "Come on, we're busy."

Norah shrugs. "I was just wondering," she says.

AVA

Nathaniel has been away on Block Island since July 5, and quite frankly, Ava is too busy with her new job at Quinns' on the Beach to miss him too much. And she certainly doesn't wish she'd gone with him. Block Island is one-tenth the size of Nantucket; it wouldn't have provided Ava with the stimulation she requires. If things with her family ever settle down to where Ava feels like she can leave Nantucket, she will go someplace bigger, not smaller. She was right to let Nathaniel go. She had had the world's shortest engagement.

When Scott got back from Tuscany, he called Ava almost immediately. "When can I see you?"

Apparently, a week in Tuscany with Roxanne hadn't been as romantic as Ava had feared.

"I was sick of her before the plane landed in Florence," Scott said. "It was a very long week. I missed you like crazy. Did you miss me?"

"Nathaniel proposed to me on the *Endeavor,*" Ava said.

Silence from Scott, which Ava savored.

"What did you say?" Scott asked.

"I said yes," Ava said.

Silence from Scott. The silence was delicious—like vanilla ice cream with hot caramel sauce, like the feel of silk sheets on her skin, like the first ocean swim of the year.

"So you're getting married?" Scott said. "Really?"

"No," Ava said. "He asked me to move to Block Island with him because he accepted a long-term job there. I said no. We broke up."

"Wow," Scott said. "For a second there, I thought I'd lost you forever."

Is Ava any closer to solving her quandary? Yes, much. She and Scott see each other nearly every night, although Ava is aware that when Scott isn't with her, he's with Roxanne. Roxanne is fragile, Scott says. And especially lately. He can't break it off completely; he's afraid of what she'll do.

Ava rolls her eyes.

She has created her finest playlist yet: a new 1980s mix—"Modern Love," by Bowie, "Tainted Love," "Life in a Northern Town." She and Kevin dance and sing into imaginary microphones as they feed the masses. Men at Work, Wham!, Loverboy. It's a good day, a very good day.

It's made even better when Ava sees Shelby in line with her baby, Xavier, strapped to her chest in a BabyBjörn.

Shelby gives Ava wide eyes and she mouths something, but Ava is bopping around to Cyndi Lauper and can't make out what Shelby is saying. When it's her turn to order, Shelby says, "I have to talk to you."

"After work?"

"No," Shelby says. "Right now. This instant."

There is an expression of extreme urgency on her best friend's face.

Bart? she thinks. Her stomach drops. But would Shelby be the one to deliver news about Bart? No.

"It can't wait?" Ava asks.

"It can't wait," Shelby says. "I'm not even hungry. I just stood in this line so I could talk to you. I've texted you ten times already."

"Okay, meet me out back," Ava says. She grabs Kevin. "Watch the register for a minute?"

"Wha—" he says.

"Please," Ava says.

Out behind the shack, Shelby reaches out to hold both of Ava's hands. Xavier is fast asleep against her chest; his tiny lips make a sucking motion.

"Roxanne Oliveria…" Shelby says.

"Roxanne?" Ava says. "Did something happen?"

"She's pregnant," Shelby says.

That night, Ava is supposed to meet Scott at the Boarding House. They have plans to eat at the bar and then go to the Chicken Box to see Scott's favorite band, Maxxtone. An hour before they're supposed to meet, Scott calls.

He says, "I have to cancel."

Ava has been thinking about how to handle this. She has decided to play dumb and let Scott lead the way. She says, "Really? How come?"

"Ava?" Scott exhales a long breath. "I'm going to be a father."

I'm going to be a father. This statement tells Ava everything she needs to know. It doesn't matter that Scott is in love with Ava; it doesn't matter that he was planning on breaking up with Roxanne. Scott has a set of values made from solid gold. He always does the upstanding, honorable thing. Plus, he has always wanted a child, three children, ten children. He's going to marry Roxanne and he is going to be a father. Ava can't stand in his way.

"I'm sorry, Ava," he says. They have to stop, cold turkey, he says. He can't see her one-on-one ever again.

Devastation. Heartbreak. Loneliness.

Ava calls Shelby and cries over the phone. She tells Kevin the news and he gives her the next day off work. She drives out to the beach at Ram Pasture with a bottle of wine and a bag of peanut butter–filled pretzels. The beach is deserted—it's the best-kept secret on the island—and this gives Ava the freedom to scream at the ocean and throw her pretzels to the seagulls. Roxanne is pregnant. Scott is going to marry her. Nathaniel is in Block Island, by now probably dating somebody else, some lucky Block Island girl that he met at the Oar, the bar that's apparently the place everybody goes. Nathaniel has asked Ava to come visit, but she has declined. Until yesterday, she had been happy with Scott. She had chosen Scott, and Scott had chosen her.

That's over now.

Scott will marry Roxanne, a woman he couldn't tolerate for seven days even in the picturesque countryside of Italy, a woman who wears high-heeled, fur-lined boots and requests "Brown-Eyed Girl" everywhere there's music playing. Ava pours herself a plastic cup of wine even though it's only three o'clock in the afternoon. She used to have two boy-friends; now she has none. It serves her right. She toasts that old bitch Karma and drinks. There is today's pain, which is bad, but she understands that today's pain will pale in comparison to the pain she will feel when she bumps into Roxanne at the grocery store and is confronted with Roxanne's burgeoning belly or when she sees the birth announcement in the *Inquirer and Mirror* or when, years from now, she sees Scott and his son or daughter having an ice cream at the soda counter of Nantucket Pharmacy.

There are emotional landmines everywhere, but there are also pragmatic landmines. It's three days before Margaret and Drake's wedding, and now Ava doesn't have a date. All of the wedding-guest numbers include Scott; without him, the event will be lopsided, off balance, or so Ava convinces herself. She is so desperate that she considers asking Scott if he will break his cold-turkey rule and escort her to the wedding and reception out of mercy; he can tell Roxanne he was grandfathered in. Next, she considers calling Nathaniel and begging him to come from Block Island, but she immediately realizes this is unfair, bordering on cruel. She could always suck it up and go alone.

When she walks out of Flowers on Chestnut carrying the box that holds her mother's bridal bouquet as well as the bouquet that she, Ava, will be carrying as maid of honor, she hears someone call her name.

She turns but can't identify the source of the voice. Town is packed. There are people everywhere—parents, children, grandparents, dogs, college kids, and couples, couples, couples.

"Ava!"

Okay, she isn't imagining it. Male voice. She stands still.

And then, crossing the street in a diagonal she sees…she sees…a man heading straight for her. Tall, dark hair peppered with gray, blue polo shirt, blue-striped shorts. It's… it's…

He offers her his hand. "Hi, it's Potter. Potter Lyons? I met you in Anguilla."

MARGARET

She is sixty-one years old and in two hours, she will be getting married for the second time. She would have said that the details of her wedding didn't matter, anything was fine—and yet, with two hours left, she finds that things matter very much. She is wearing an ivory gown designed for her by Donna Karan that is possibly more flattering to her figure than her original wedding dress was, even though she'd worn that one at the age of twenty-three. She doesn't want to make comparisons like that—first wedding versus second wedding— because after nearly forty years, so much has changed. She's a different person.

But she is still, apparently, type A. She relaxes only once Patrick, Jennifer, and the boys have arrived, and she puts her hands on the sides of Patrick's face and gives her firstborn a kiss.

"You have no idea how good it is to see you," she says.

"I have every idea," Patrick says. "I love you, Mom. Thank you for not giving up on me."

"Oh, honey," she says. For a second, she is speechless. Is she thrilled that Patrick broke the law and went to jail? Obviously not. But she knows him well enough to realize that he has learned his lesson and he'll bounce back just fine. As for her giving up on him, well...he has three boys of his own, so he understands that no parent ever gives up on his or her child.

Patrick says, "I can't believe you gave Dad my job. I thought *I* would give you away."

"Your poor father," Margaret says. "He's earned it."

The ceremony is simple but that doesn't mean it's uncomplicated. There are two dozen white chairs lined up on the beach, twelve on each side with a sandy aisle between. At the end of the aisle is the altar—a white arched trellis dripping with roses. There is a harp, a cello, and a trumpet, and Gordon Russell to sing. When all of the guests are seated—including George's girlfriend, Mary Rose, wearing a remarkably large hat—Darcy, Margaret's assistant and de facto wedding planner, gives the signal, and the harpist and cellist launch into Pachelbel's Canon in D.

Ava, Kelley, and Margaret are standing on top of the dune, watching the action below. Ava advances down the aisle, looking beautiful in a pink silk sheath that is exactly the color of her flushed cheeks.

"Do you think she's okay?" Margaret asks Kelley. Ava broke it off with Nathaniel back in June, and then only a week ago she and Scott broke up when it turned out that he'd gotten the other woman he was dating pregnant. Miraculously, Ava bumped into Potter Lyons, the nice young man she and Margaret met in Anguilla, and now he's here as Ava's date. Potter seems perfectly at home despite the fact that he knows exactly nobody; he is sitting with Kevin and Isabelle and Genevieve. Genevieve is old enough to stand on Kevin's lap, and when she's standing, she grabs Potter's ear, but he doesn't seem to mind. His eyes are glued to Ava as she proceeds down the aisle; Margaret can decipher the expression on his face even from a hundred yards away. He's smitten.

"Now is not the time to worry about Ava," Kelley says. "Now is the time to worry about yourself."

But Margaret doesn't have any worries. She is marrying a man she is madly, hopelessly in love with, a man she respects, a man she enjoys. When the music changes to Jeremiah Clarke's Trumpet Voluntary, she and Kelley take their first steps forward. Margaret's gaze is fixed on Drake, so handsome in his tuxedo at the altar. But she can also see the years of her future unfurling before her, and they are all golden.

KEVIN

He's been watching Jennifer, paying closer attention to her than he has in all the years he's known her. Is she thinner? Is she manic? Is she sluggish? Are her hands shaking? Are her pupils constricted? She seems the same, but he feels like he's missing something. Her hair is longer; it looks nice.

Kevin remembers the first time Patrick brought Jennifer home. They had met in New York at one of the soulless bars on the Upper East Side—not J. G. Melon's or Dorrian's, but someplace like it. What Kevin recalls is how Jack-and-Jill Patrick and Jennifer were, like male and female versions of the same person. Not in how they looked, certainly—Patrick has red hair and a doughy face, whereas Jennifer has coalblack hair and sharp features—but in how they acted, how they viewed the world, how they spoke, the things they liked to do. They both got up early to go running; they both ate twigs-and-leaves cereal topped with fresh berries and skim milk; they both read the *New York Times* like it was the lost Gospel; they both took quick, efficient showers and then made a plan, with sub-plans, for their day. Kevin had thought he'd never come across anyone as anal as Patrick—until he met Jennifer. Together, they were almost too much, with their achieving and their problem-solving, their loquaciousness, their eagerness to discuss this foreign film, that Argentinean steak house, if Franzen was losing his touch, what the best use of forty million Starwood points was, which was higher on the bucket list—New Orleans for Jazz Fest or the Kentucky Derby? *They're going to implode,* Kevin used to think, *like a star.* The couple they most reminded him of was Kelley and Margaret just before the divorce—back when Kelley had a cocaine habit and Margaret was consumed with breaking through the glass ceiling in broadcast journalism.

But Paddy and Jennifer had made it, an impressive feat, especially considering this most recent set of circumstances— indictment, jail time, public humiliation, and separation for eighteen months.

Maybe Jennifer *did* buy pills from Norah once or twice— could anyone blame her?—but she certainly isn't an addict. This isn't something Kevin needs to worry about.

The ceremony is stunning in its elegant simplicity. Margaret walks barefoot through the sand in her ivory gown with her famous red hair swept up in a chignon, decorated in the back with a single white calla lily. Drake grins like he's the luckiest man on earth, which he most certainly is. Kelley hands Margaret over at the altar, but first he gives Margaret a hug. Kevin has never cried at a wedding in his life, but he feels tears prick his eyes when he sees the embrace between his mother and his father. They were married for twenty years. They had three kids and a brownstone in New York City and friends and traditions and a life together. And although that life didn't last, here they are: friends, best friends, more than best friends. They love each other; they want each other to be happy.

It's a beautiful thing, Kevin thinks, the relationship between his parents. Anyone can fall in love, but not just anyone can achieve forgiveness and acceptance and real, deep respect for his or her former partner the way those two have.

Kevin would never give Norah Vale away. Nope, not in a trillion lifetimes.

After the ceremony, there's a reception on the beach. Kevin had offered to cater it, but Margaret didn't want him working on her wedding day. She hired Nantucket Catering Company to do an old-fashioned beach picnic: hamburgers, hot dogs, fried chicken, potato salad, deviled eggs, pickles, watermelon, and grilled corn on the cob. Patrick has brought a football that he throws to his sons at the waterline.

Genevieve is being passed around. Everyone wants a chance to hold her, which gives Kevin the opportunity to make a plate. When he turns around to sit, he can't find Isabelle. He sees Mitzi talking to George and Mary Rose; Ava introducing her date, Potter, to Lee Kramer, the head of CBS; Kelley chatting with Shelby and Zack. He notices Jennifer heading up over the dune by herself, which is odd. Maybe Isabelle has gone that way too? Kevin checks on Genevieve—Margaret's assistant, Darcy, is holding her. Kevin sets down his plate and trails Jennifer.

When he crests the dune, he sees Jennifer on her phone. He can tell by her body language that this is a clandestine call, and whereas normally, Kevin would give Jennifer her privacy, today he gets right up on her.

"Okay," Jennifer says. "I'll see you tomorrow at nine at your place."

She hangs up, and when she turns around, Kevin is in her face. She gasps and nearly loses her grip on the phone.

"Kevin!" she says.

"Who was that?" Kevin asks.

"Excuse me?" Jennifer says.

"Who were you on the phone with?"

Jennifer's expression travels from shocked to indignant with a brief detour through fear. Kevin sees the fear, just a flicker, and knows she's hiding something.

"Nobody," she says.

"Nobody," he says. He stares at her, wondering if she thinks he's going to accept that answer.

"None of your business, I mean," she says.

"You're meeting someone at nine tomorrow," he says. "Who are you meeting?"

"It's not what you think," Jennifer says.

"What do I think?" he says.

"I'm not having an affair," she says. "I would never."

Kevin is temporarily stymied. He supposes if he hadn't heard the rumor about Norah and he'd stumbled across Jennifer having that conversation, he might have thought affair.

"Who was it, then?" he asks.

Before Jennifer can answer, Kevin hears crying and he looks around. About a hundred yards away, on the back side of the next dune, Kevin sees Isabelle sitting by herself, her face buried in her hands. It's Isabelle who is crying.

Kevin gives Jennifer a stern look. "I'm not finished with you," he says.

Kevin supposes that every wedding has its drama. Isabelle is crying because her heart is breaking, despite the fact that Margaret and Drake's wedding is so beautiful and an occasion for celebration, or maybe due to that. Isabelle and Kevin have been engaged a year longer than Margaret and Drake; they have a child who is about to celebrate her first birthday, and they still aren't married. Isabelle's parents—devout Catholics—are scandalized. They have been waiting and waiting for Isabelle to tell them the date and send them tickets to America so they can see their grandchild. It is understood that they will come only once—on the occasion of Isabelle's wedding.

"Oh, sweetheart," Kevin says. "I'm so sorry. I've been such an idiot!" Kevin has noticed how subdued Isabelle is after her weekly call to her parents in Marseille, but he assumed that was because she missed them. He never considered that they might be asking her questions she isn't comfortable answering, such as *When will you be getting married? When will your baby be legitimate?* Kevin has been so wrapped up with his own family that he never considered Isabelle's family.

He hasn't proposed any dates for the wedding because he has been waiting until Bart comes home. But now he sees that waiting for Bart might mean waiting forever.

"Let's get married at Christmas," Kevin says. "Christmas Eve at the inn, two years to the day after I proposed. How does that sound?"

Isabelle gives him a tiny smile. *"Vraiment?"*

"Yes, really," Kevin says. "I'll buy tickets for your parents tomorrow." He loves that he now has the money to make such an offer. He takes Isabelle's hand. "Will you marry me, Isabelle? Will you marry me on Christmas Eve?"

"Yes," she says.

AVA

Margaret had described it as an "old person's wedding" in that the whole event would be over by nine o'clock. Initially, Ava had counted this as a good thing; she'd need to hang with Potter for only four hours. But within minutes, she remembers why she likes this guy. He's witty and articulate. He listens. And he is thrilled to be here, escorting Ava to her mother's wedding. He doesn't mind that Ava picked him up off the street and gave him less than twenty-four hours' notice. He went right to Murray's and bought a navy blazer and a Vineyard Vines tie.

"I can't believe my luck," Potter says. "I thought about stopping by at the inn when I got on island, but since you never sent my hat, I figured you'd forgotten about me."

Ava gasps. "I never sent your hat!" She had gotten home from Anguilla and was sucked right back into her real life—Scott/Nathaniel/Nathaniel/Scott—and whatever flirtation she'd engaged in on the vacation evaporated. She had thought of Potter fleetingly a couple of times, but not long enough to remember that she owed him a hat.

Margaret and Drake cut the cake at eight o'clock and by eight thirty, they're walking hand in hand over the path to where a dune buggy awaits to take them to an undisclosed location for the night.

Potter looks at Ava. "Are we going home, or are we going out?"

"Out," she says, surprising herself. "Let's go out."

Kevin and Isabelle take Genevieve home, and Zack and Shelby do the same with Xavier. Mitzi and Kelley take Paddy's three boys and they invite George and Mary Rose to join them for a nightcap back at the inn.

"Who's the woman in the hat?" Potter asks Ava.

"Mary Rose," Ava says. "George's girlfriend."

"And who is George?" Potter asks.

"He's..." Ava isn't sure how to explain. "He's our Santa Claus at the inn every year."

"Ohhh...kay," Potter says.

Margaret's assistant, Darcy, and Drake's nephew, Liam, are young enough that they want to go to Straight Wharf, but Ava is dressed in a silk sheath and all she can picture is someone spilling a Goombay Smash down the front of it. She lobbies for someplace more adult. She and Potter and Patrick and Jennifer decide to go to the Summer House in Sconset. The Summer House has an old-time-Nantucket feel that Ava loves. There's a piano player and a log burning in the fireplace and exposed beams and overstuffed chairs.

"I never do this," Ava says once she settles down to order, "but I'll have a martini. Dirty."

"Me too!" Jennifer says, and Ava laughs. She has noticed a huge change in Jennifer since Paddy's been back. She is joyous; she is loose.

After the first martini, which goes down way too easily, Ava and Jennifer excuse themselves and head to the ladies' room.

Immediately, Jennifer grabs Ava's arm. "I love him!" she says.

"Who?" Ava says.

"Potter!" Jennifer says. "He's the best! He's so smart! He's an academic, but he's not stuffy. He's funny. And he's worldly! He's been everywhere on that sailboat. And he has emotional depth. That story about losing his parents and being raised by his grandparents had me in tears. He loves his grandfather."

"Gibby," Ava says. Potter has mentioned Gibby twice that

evening. Apparently, Gibby isn't doing well, and Potter is worried about him. It does give him soul, Ava thinks, the way he is so attached to his grandparents, sailing around in a sloop named after his grandmother. And he is smart, intellectual even—but without making Ava feel stupid. "I don't know. When I met him, I thought he was too good-looking."

"So you're not going to date him because he's too good-looking?" Jennifer says. "He is so into you! You should have seen the way he watched you when you walked down the aisle."

Ava blushes. She did catch his eye for an instant, almost by accident.

"You should marry Potter," Jennifer declares.

They've just come from a wedding, so obviously marriage is on everyone's mind, but for some reason, Jennifer's comment hits Ava the wrong way. It might be the vodka, or it might be the fact that, right after he delivered Margaret to the altar, Kelley sat down next to Ava and whispered, "I can't wait to walk you down the aisle."

Honestly! Ava thinks. It's as if Ava won't count as a person until she has settled down with a husband!

"I'm not marrying Potter Lyons," Ava says to her sister-in-law. "I'm not marrying anybody."

From the Summer House, they take a taxi to the Bar, where Maxxtone is playing. It's Scott's favorite band, but Ava tries not to dwell on this as they walk in. They are able to sidle in through the back door, avoiding the long line, because Kevin managed the Bar for almost a decade.

"Wow," Potter says. "In all the years I've been coming here, I've never been able to pull this off."

Patrick slaps Potter on the back. While Ava and Jennifer were in the bathroom at the Summer House, Patrick and Potter found they had half a million friends and acquaintances in common, the most amazing discovery being that Potter was a fraternity brother of Patrick's boss, Great Guy Gary Grimstead. And Potter has sailed with guys who went to Columbia Business School with Patrick. Ava begins to see Potter as just another version of her older brother, but then Potter takes her hand as he leads her through the crowd at the Bar. It's the first time he's touched her all evening, and although the circumstances couldn't be more different, Ava has an instant sense memory of walking along the sand in Anguilla and the three kisses on the beached Sunfish. Potter must be having the exact same memories because he stops and pulls Ava close to him. He takes her face in his hands and he bends down to kiss her. It's wonderful. They are surrounded on all sides by people drinking and laughing. The Bar is pulsing with live music, and Ava feels young and wild for a second. It's late, she's drunk, and she's kissing a near-perfect stranger. It's been a while since she has experienced this particular trifecta.

Potter stops kissing her as Patrick approaches with their beers.

"Don't let me interrupt," he says.

Ava accepts her beer. Out of the corner of her eye, she sees a guy sitting at the bar who looks like Scott.

Is it Scott? His shoulders are hunched and he appears to be holding his head off the bar with his palm. His eyes are at half-mast. In front of him is a highball glass of brown liquid. Ava blinks; she doesn't trust her eyes. Could that be Scott, visibly drunk and looking like Eeyore with a whiskey in front of him? She has never known Scott to drink whiskey. He's a three-beers-and-done man.

It's not Scott, she tells herself. And even if it were Scott, they've ended the relationship cold turkey, and so it's not as though she can go up and say hello. Nope, even that is off-limits. But it can't be Scott, because what would Scott be doing at the Bar at midnight when Roxanne is at home, pregnant with their child?

"Do you know the guy in the green shirt?" Potter asks. "He's staring at you."

"Kiss me again," Ava says.

Potter doesn't have to be asked twice.

Ava breaks away, breathless. "Let's go dance," she says.

GEORGE

When Mitzi told George that Margaret Quinn's boss was married to the editor of *Vogue* and that both would be attending the wedding, he knew he had to RSVP yes, despite Mary Rose's objections.

"I feel funny," Mary Rose had said when the invitation arrived. "This is the wedding of my boyfriend's ex-girlfriend's husband's ex-wife, who also happens to be Margaret Quinn. Do I belong?"

George had wondered himself at the source of the invitation. After much pondering, he decided Mitzi had been behind it. The invitation was a peace offering and to turn away an olive branch would mean twenty years of bad luck. They were all adults. George and Mitzi had conducted an affair every Christmas for twelve years, but when they tried to make their relationship work full-time, it had fallen apart. In a way, George's failings with Mitzi were what had led her back to Kelley. Plus, he could say that he was one of very few non–family members to attend Margaret Quinn's wedding.

Yes, they had to go. And George would design Mary Rose the hat of a lifetime.

They wouldn't stay at the inn, George decided. That would be too awkward, returning to the lodging and possibly even the room where Mitzi had secretly come to visit him for so many years. Instead, George booked a room at the Castle, down the street. The Castle had a large, brand-new fitness center, which was a bonus, as both George and Mary Rose have been on a health kick since the first of the year. George has lost nearly thirty pounds. By Christmas, he hopes to be a very skinny Santa indeed.

All of George's gambles have paid off. The night before the wedding, George and Mary Rose wander the streets of town. It's the first time Mary Rose has been to the island in the summer. They stroll the docks and ogle the great yachts that are in Nantucket for Race Week. They have a romantic dinner on the beach at the Galley. And then, in the morning, at Mitzi's invitation, they swing by the inn to enjoy one of Kelley's famous breakfasts—lobster eggs Benedict, made especially for the wedding guests.

George had feared the initial interaction with Kelley and Mitzi would be strained—there was nothing like welcoming your wife's former lover into the fold!—but it was surprisingly joyous. Kelley and Mitzi greeted George and Mary Rose like old friends; a stranger watching might have thought George and Kelley had once been college roommates or that the four of them had forged a lifelong bond on a cruise to Alaska.

And the hat! Well, the hat makes quite a splash. No sooner has Mary Rose taken her seat at the ceremony than a murmur ripples through the assembled guests. They are talking about the hat—a classic boater made from finely braided leghorn straw with a twelve-inch brim and a lime-green satin band that trails halfway down Mary Rose's back. At the reception, Mary Rose is approached by none other than Ginny Kramer, the editor of *Vogue,* who asks who designed the hat.

"Why, my boyfriend, George Umbrau," Mary Rose says as she tugs on George's arm. "He's a milliner."

"I'd love to feature his hats in the magazine," Ginny says. She hands George her card. "Send me a few samples?"

"Of course!" George says. He can't believe his good fortune. His hat business has just hit a plateau after two years of upswing, thanks to a selection in Oprah's Favorite Things, and he's been wondering how to reinvigorate sales. A feature or even a mention in *Vogue* will do the trick. He is in his late sixties and ready to retire. He would like to sell his business to a large retailer such as Talbots or Ann Taylor, and he'd like to get a good price so that he and Mary Rose can travel the globe in style.

After the wedding reception, George and Mary Rose catch a ride back to town with Kelley and Mitzi, and George tells them about his stroke of good fortune.

"It's not good fortune," Kelley says. "She recognizes your talent."

George can't believe how generous Kelley is being with his praise. He feels almost embarrassed.

"They're beautiful hats, George," Mitzi says. George thinks about how Mitzi had gamely tried on several styles before admitting to him that she hated to wear hats. He had known then that things would never work out between them. Mary Rose is a woman who would sleep in a hat if she could.

"Well, thank you both," George says as Kelley pulls up outside the Castle. "It was a most delightful evening."

"Yes," Mary Rose says. "Thank you for including us."

"The pleasure was ours," Kelley says. He gets out of the

car to help Mary Rose to the curb and to shake George's hand. "I want to let bygones be bygones. I don't see why the four of us can't be friends. Would you guys consider coming back and staying with us at Christmas? Maybe don the red suit one more time?"

"I'd love to," George says. He can't believe how happy the offer makes him. He dresses as Santa for a variety of Lions Club events in Lenox but nothing gives him more pleasure than playing Santa on Nantucket.

"With your new svelte physique, you'll have to get the suit altered," Kelley says.

"Or I could fatten him up by Christmas," Mary Rose says, and she and Mitzi laugh.

As Kelley and Mitzi drive away, Mary Rose and George wave good-bye, then George leads Mary Rose by the hand up the stairs of the Castle. He imagines his hats being featured in the windows of Bergdorf Goodman.

"They're such a nice couple," Mary Rose says. "I can't believe you nearly broke them up. Shame on you, George."

JENNIFER

At eight o'clock the morning after Margaret and Drake's wedding, despite a tremendous hangover, Jennifer laces up her running shoes.

Patrick rolls over in bed and tugs on her shirt. "Don't go," he says. "Come back to bed."

She turns around and smiles, but even that small effort feels like it's enough to crack her face in half. After Ava saw Scott at the Bar, she and Jennifer ordered Fireball shots.

What a rotten idea! And it had been Jennifer's. "I'll be back between nine thirty and ten."

"Not only a run, but a long run," Patrick says. "You go, girl."

Jennifer hopes to slip out of the inn unnoticed, but she bumps into Kevin on the back stairs.

Kevin. Of all people.

"Hey!" he says. He checks his watch. "Where are you off to?"

Jennifer tugs on her tank top. "Going for a run," she says. She wonders if Kevin remembers the conversation they had the evening before. Did he tuck away the particulars? He's looking at her strangely, with his head cocked, as if he's trying to see her from another angle. He thinks she's having an affair; Jennifer would bet her life on it. Well, let him think that. In some ways, it's preferable to the truth. "I'm off," she says.

"Enjoy!" Kevin says.

She goes out the back door of the inn and heads down Liberty Street to Gardner. She figures it'll take her forty minutes to run to Norah Vale's house, ten minutes to do the deal, and forty minutes to run home.

She needs more drugs. She has been trying to wean herself off the oxy and at one point, when Patrick was first home, she had made it through an entire day with only one pill. But after that, she felt moody and headachy and sick and she deeply craved the high of the oxy, the sense of order and focus it brought her. She couldn't live without it. Could not, would not. She had met Norah once in July at their usual spot on Route 3, thinking that would be it. But now that she's on Nantucket where Norah *lives,* the temptation is too great to resist. She's going to buy sixty pills. These sixty will be the end, she tells herself. But she has to get these sixty. The mere thought of so many pills puts her at peace.

Norah had been surprised to hear from Jennifer, or possibly she had only been acting surprised. She knows Jennifer is an addict, and as much as Jennifer would like to blame Norah and think her evil, Jennifer can't blame anyone but herself. She wishes she had found a dealer who didn't know her; the connection between her and Norah makes her very uneasy. When Jennifer called two days ago to say she would be on the island, Norah said, "Family vacation?"

Without thinking, Jennifer said, "Margaret is getting married, actually."

"Really?" Norah said. She then pressed Jennifer for details, and what could Jennifer do but comply? Dr. Drake Carroll, pediatric neurosurgeon, ceremony on the beach at Eel Point, Kelley giving Margaret away. It was confidential information—no one wanted the paparazzi to show up—but Margaret had once been Norah's mother-in-law, and if Jennifer remembered correctly, Norah had been fond of Margaret. And Margaret had been kind and gracious with Norah because Margaret was kind and gracious with everyone.

"Wow," Norah said wistfully. "I bet it will be a beautiful wedding."

Jennifer actually felt bad that Norah hadn't been invited—which was crazy. The only thing that could confuse and frustrate you more than family was . . . former family.

Jennifer jogs into the driveway of the Vale family compound at five minutes to nine. Jennifer has been here only once, years and years earlier, when Kevin and Norah were still married. The compound is off Hooper Farm Road—it's mid-island, where the island businesses are and where the locals live. There are four vehicles in the driveway: Norah's black truck; an old Jeep Wagoneer, its bumper plastered with beach stickers; and two old taxis, one of which is on blocks, that Jennifer knows used to belong to Norah's parents. Also in the driveway are two rusted-out bikes, a sun-bleached Big Wheel, half of a brass bed, a pile of scallop shells that stinks to high heaven, and a deflated kiddie pool.

A German shepherd fights its chain in the backyard, barking an announcement of Jennifer Barrett Quinn's arrival at the low point in her life. She puts her hands on her hips and bends in half to catch her breath. She closes her eyes, but even the black is splotched blood red. *Turn around,* she thinks. *You don't need the drugs.*

She does need the drugs.

Norah comes bouncing out of the house wearing...here, Jennifer blinks. Norah is wearing a Lilly Pulitzer shift dress. It's light pink patterned with hot-pink flamingos playing croquet and it has white curlicue appliqué down the front that looks like icing on a birthday cake. The neckline is high enough to cover Norah's terrifying python tattoo. Norah's hair is in a French braid and she's wearing pearl earrings and white Jack Rogers sandals. The transformation of Norah Vale is complete; she is indistinguishable from any of the women who lean over the railing of the party yacht *Belle* holding gin and tonics.

"You look great," Jennifer says.

"Thanks," Norah says. She gives Jennifer a shy smile. "I'm having lunch with one of my clients at the Wauwinet today."

This statement pulls Jennifer up short. The Wauwinet! Even Jennifer and Patrick don't splurge on lunch at the Wauwinet. And when Norah says "client," she means...another woman she sells drugs to, right? It seems wrong somehow. Jennifer is an interior designer; *she* has clients. Then Jennifer realizes that, in some ways, she and Norah are doing the same thing. Jennifer is selling women Persian rugs and nautical prints, antique chests and silk drapes—things they don't need but that they buy for the high, she supposes, the high of owning beautiful things.

Jennifer can't dwell on this. *She* is not a drug dealer. And yet, any favorable comparison of herself with Norah fails at this moment. Norah looks successful and put together, whereas Jennifer looks like a sweating, jonesing junkie.

She pulls a wad of cash out of the back zipped pocket of her Lululemon shorts. "Here you go."

Norah hands over the pills, this time in a jar of multivitamins. Smart girl; she knows Jennifer is going back to the inn.

Jennifer takes the pills and feels a wave of relief and elation and all-is-right-with-the-world. Sixty pills.

Norah's eyes float over Jennifer's right shoulder and before Jennifer can do anything more than blink, Norah turns and runs.

Jennifer swivels her head to see Kevin's white pickup pull into the driveway.

Did he follow her here? Jennifer wonders. Instinctively, she tucks the vitamins into her waistband. She will come up with an explanation.

Kevin gets out of the pickup. And then...so does Patrick.

No, Jennifer thinks. *No, this isn't happening.*

"Jennifer?" Patrick says.

AVA

She and Potter dance in the front row of the Bar until closing. The band plays "Add It Up" by the Violent Femmes as their last song but then the crowd chants, "One more song!"

One more song!" and the band obliges and plays "Just Like Heaven" by the Cure. Potter spins Ava around and dips her and she is as carefree as she has ever been in her life.

"Let's go find your brother," Potter says.

"I'm sure he left," Ava says. Patrick is the responsible stick-in-the-mud of the family. There's no way he's still hanging around the Bar at one thirty in the morning.

As Ava and Potter weave and wend their way through the crowd, someone grabs Ava's arm.

It's Scott.

"Can I talk to you for a second?" he asks.

Before Ava can answer, Potter steps in. "Hi there," he says. "I'm Potter Lyons. Is there a problem?"

"No *problem*," Scott says. His lip curls in a way that makes him seem surly. What is *wrong* with him? Ava is pretty sure Scott has never struck anyone as surly in all his life. "I'd just like a chance to talk to my girlfriend, if you don't mind."

Potter holds his palms up and takes a step back.

Ava says, "Your *girlfriend?* I am no longer your *girlfriend,* Scott. Your *girlfriend* is at home, pregnant with your *child*."

"Whoa," Potter says. "I'll be at the bar. I'm going to grab a glass of water. Come find me."

He disappears and Ava glances up at Scott. He still doesn't look like himself. "I can't do this right now, Scott, I'm sorry."

"I need to talk to you. I need to tell you something. Something bad."

"Whatever it is, I don't want to hear it," Ava says.

"But—" Scott says.

Ava raises a hand like a traffic cop. "This is what cold turkey feels like, Scott. Cold."

At the bar, Ava finds Potter with Jennifer. Potter hands Ava an ice water.

"You saw Scott?" Jennifer says. "What did he want?"

What did Scott—or Nathaniel, for that matter—always want? They wanted to make Ava's life tumultuous and confusing. It was as if they waited until Ava was relaxed and actually enjoying herself before they pitched the next curveball.

Ava shrugs. Jennifer signals the bartender. "Two shots of Fireball," she says.

Patrick offers to drive Ava and Potter home, but Ava says no, thank you. She and Potter will take a cab.

When they are finally alone in the quiet of the backseat, Ava says, "Thank you for a truly wonderful evening. It's not everybody who could attend an intimate family wedding for a very famous woman at the last minute and rock it like you did."

Potter laughs. "The pleasure was mine, I assure you."

The taxi delivers them to Old North Wharf. Potter is staying on his sailboat, *Cassandra*.

"Would you like a tour?" Potter asks. "Or a nightcap?"

She's not surprised he's asking; it's the natural way to end their night—with some good old-fashioned making out that may or may not turn into rollicking boat sex.

But Ava can't do it.

She reaches her arms around Potter's neck and gives him a kiss on each cheek. She still thinks he's too handsome for her, and now she knows he's also socially savvy, oodles of fun, and a better dancer than Nathaniel and Scott put together. But she doesn't have the energy for another relationship or even a one-night stand. The run-in with Scott has left her addled.

"Thank you for tonight," she says.

He nods slowly, understanding her. "How will you get home?"

"I'll walk," she says. "I need to clear my head."

He holds her face and gives her one soft but insistent kiss on the lips, and immediately Ava remembers the desire she felt when he kissed her on the Sunfish in Anguilla. It is almost enough to flip her.

"Text me when you get home so I know you're safe," he says. "And Ava?"

She raises her eyebrows. Those blue eyes. Whoa.

"Come see me in New York."

MARGARET

She has asked for one thing, discreetly, as a wedding present from her three children, and that is a lunch at Something Natural, just the four of them. She thinks about how selfish it is for her to request this—no Drake, no Isabelle, no Jennifer, no grandchildren, no Kelley or Mitzi—but Margaret doesn't care. She wants an hour eating sandwiches in the sunshine with her children.

Not on Sunday, when everyone will be hungover and exhausted. Margaret wants to spend Sunday with Drake alone. But on Monday, at noon.

Margaret bikes to Something Natural all the way from her and Drake's hideaway in Sconset. She wears a hat and sunglasses so as not to be recognized.

Ava is already waiting for Margaret, sitting on the steps in front of the sandwich shop.

"I got us seats," she says, pointing to a picnic table tucked in the back corner of the property, partially under the shade of a giant elm.

"Shall we wait for the boys before we order?" Margaret asks. She can't believe how excited she is about this lunch date. It's the most difficult for Kevin, she knows, who has had to leave Quinns' on the Beach in the hands of his newly appointed assistant manager, Devon, two of the past three days. Both he and Ava will head to Quinns' as soon as lunch is over.

"They were right behind me," Ava says.

And sure enough, a few seconds later, Kevin's white pickup pulls into the already congested driveway; he squeezes the truck into a spot between two Range Rovers, and then both he and Patrick shimmy out through their open windows.

Patrick has lost a lot of weight in jail; Margaret noticed that on Saturday.

They all get in line and order their sandwiches. Margaret gets the Sheila's Favorite on oatmeal; Ava gets avocado, cheddar, and chutney; Kevin orders smoked turkey, Swiss, and tomato on herb bread; Patrick gets the lobster salad on pumpernickel.

Margaret adds chips, Nantucket Nectars, and four huge chocolate chip cookies to the order.

"I've had a rough twenty-four hours," Patrick says.

"The kids?" Margaret asks.

"The wife," Patrick says.

"Jennifer?" Margaret says.

"She's the only wife I have," Patrick says. "Although there were some guys in prison who wanted the job." He smiles wanly. "I'm kidding. It wasn't that kind of prison. And if it were, I wouldn't tell you."

Margaret is surprised to hear that there's a problem with Jennifer. She single-handedly ran the family for a year and a half, and, as far as Margaret could tell, she did it beautifully.

She cared for the boys, kept their routines, loved and nurtured them. She stayed true to Patrick, visiting him at every chance, calling every week, sending letters and noncontraband care packages. She ran her business and held her head high in the community—and that couldn't have been easy. Patrick married Jennifer Barrett because she was strong and an achiever like him, but as Margaret has learned, it's easy to be strong when life unspools as it should—kids, house, cars, vacations, money—and another thing when the man you love lies to you and everyone else, loses his job, and disgraces his name by going to prison for fraud.

Fraud. Margaret loathes the word now. It chills her.

Margaret can't imagine Jennifer giving Patrick a rough time but if she has, she should be forgiven.

"Let's sit," she says.

The four of them settle—they unwrap their sandwiches, open chips, pop the tops off their Nectars and read the factoids on the caps.

Margaret's says: *The body of water between Martha's Vineyard and Nantucket is the Muskeget Channel.*

"I did *not* know that," she says. She hoists the bottle in a toast. "Thank you for indulging me in this one wish. I really want to catch up with the three of you before I go on my honeymoon."

They all clink bottles. Cheers.

"I want to know what's going on in your lives," Margaret says. "Little stuff, big stuff."

"Let's start with the overlooked, underappreciated middle child," Kevin says. "Isabelle and I have set a date for our wedding."

"Hold on," Ava says. "I thought you were going to wait until Bart got home."

"Yeah," Patrick says. "You should wait, man."

"I can't wait," Kevin says. "It's not fair to Isabelle. Or to Genevieve."

"But…" Ava says.

"Ava," Kevin says. "We don't know when Bart is coming home." He stares at his turkey sandwich. "We don't know *if* Bart is coming home."

They all sit in silence with that for a second and Margaret thinks about how incredibly gracious it was for Kelley and Mitzi to host her and Drake's wedding when their son is still missing. Back in December, with the news that William Burke was still alive, the family's optimism peaked, but Burke still isn't far enough along in his recovery to shed any light on the location of the other soldiers.

"When is the date?" Margaret asks, laying a hand on Kevin's arm.

"Christmas Eve," Kevin says. "Isabelle's parents will fly in from France."

"A Christmas wedding," Margaret says. "It's a beautiful idea. Have you told your father?"

"Not yet," Kevin says.

"He's not going to like it," Ava says. "He'll probably think you're giving up on Bart. Mitzi most definitely will."

"I'm sorry, Ava," Kevin says. "I mean no disrespect to Bart, but I have to consider the women in my life."

"Drake and I will plan to come for Christmas, then," Margaret says. She takes a bite of her sandwich, then wipes her mouth and says, "And who knows? Bart might be home before that."

Ava looks like she's teetering on the knife-edge of tears. "Another wedding," she says.

Margaret says, "Potter certainly was a lot of fun."

Ava shrugs.

Kevin nudges her. "Yeah, maybe Potter's the one."

"I'm taking some time alone," Ava says. "No Nathaniel, no Scott, no Potter. No wedding on the horizon for me. Everyone is just going to have to love me for who I am."

"Oh, honey," Margaret says. "We do love you for who you are. We always have and we always will."

"Speaking of Scott," Patrick says, "Jenny said he tried to talk to you at the Bar the other night."

"Yeah," Ava says.

"Scott was at the Bar?" Margaret says. "Was he with Roxanne? Was she drinking? That seems pretty risky for a pregnant woman."

"He was alone," Ava says. "I refused to talk to him. But Shelby called me this morning to tell me that Roxanne miscarried."

"Oh no!" Margaret says. "I'm so sorry for her."

"Are *you* sorry for her?" Kevin asks Ava.

"Of course I'm sorry for her!" Ava says. "I'm sure Scott is crushed. He was put on this earth to be a father. And now he and Roxanne have broken things off."

Margaret takes a bite of her sandwich. She wonders if that means Ava and Scott will start seeing each other again, but she knows better than to ask. In the former matchup between Nathaniel and Scott, Margaret was on Team Scott. Scott is responsible, solid, steady, and clearly besotted with Ava, whereas Nathaniel seems a little more like Peter Pan and a little more cavalier with Ava's affections. Margaret had frankly been shocked when Scott started dating the hot-to-trot English teacher.

Patrick says, "Well, I have some news, but it's not very good."

Kevin says, "Paddy, man, this is neither the time nor the place."

Patrick shrugs. He lifts his sunglasses to the top of his head so Margaret can see his whole face. There are crow's-feet around his eyes; he looks old. And if her child looks old, what does that mean for Margaret? Nothing good, she's sure.

"What is it, honey?" she says.

"Jennifer is addicted to pills," Patrick says. "Oxy and Ativan."

"Oh, Paddy," Margaret says. Immediately, Margaret flashes back to this past December, Stroll weekend, the lunch at the Sea Grille after Genevieve's baptism. Jennifer had become completely unhinged, and Margaret had thought—hadn't she?—that Jennifer seemed like she was on something. Her behavior had reminded Margaret of Kelley back in the late eighties when he was snorting cocaine night and day.

"You're kidding!" Ava says. "Jennifer? I always thought Jennifer was . . . I don't know . . . perfect."

"That's the problem," Patrick says. "Everyone always thought both of us were perfect. Then I proved I wasn't, and Jennifer—well, she's human too. She needed something to help her cope. Her friend Megan, the one who had breast cancer, gave her a couple of Ativan to take the edge off, then a couple of oxy to pep her up. And when those were gone, Jennifer found a dealer."

"A dealer?" Ava says. "I can't believe you just used the words *Jennifer* and *dealer* in the same sentence."

Margaret noticed Kevin bow his head.

"It gets worse," Patrick says.

Margaret finishes the first half of her sandwich. She's not sure she wants to hear about worse.

"Her dealer is Norah."

"Norah?" Ava says. "Norah *Vale?*"

Good God, Margaret thinks. She closes her eyes and wishes she were back on the porch of her and Drake's romantic, rose-covered cottage in Sconset, enjoying blissful ignorance.

FALL

KELLEY

Columbus Day marks the end of the busy season and Kelley plans a leaf-peeping trip for Mitzi to take her mind off the fact that ten months have passed and not only has there been no new information about Bart but the doctors at Walter Reed National Military Medical Center are reporting that Private William Burke is suffering from memory loss. Kelley would like to quiz the doctors himself. How much memory loss? Can he answer the most basic of questions: *Are the other soldiers alive?* Will his memory ever come back? Has he handed over *any* intelligence about where he was being held? Hasn't modern medicine advanced enough that the doctors can tease information from Private Burke's mind? Isn't there some kind of sophisticated, secret mind-reading software?

Bart!

Kelley and Mitzi read the news about Private Burke's amnesia together, Kelley scanning Mitzi's expression, searching for a clue to her reaction.

She is quiet for a while, then says, in a matter-of-fact tone that shocks Kelley, "It might have been so awful he blocked it."

Together, they sigh.

Mitzi's general demeanor has improved by leaps and bounds

since she moved back in. The time in Lenox with George proved to her how much she loved Kelley. When Kelley was given a clean bill of health, Mitzi began living in a state of sustained gratitude. She now practices yoga daily, engages with the guests, and is willing to leave the inn to go on dates and outings with Kelley. They have hiked Sanford Farm; they have slurped oysters at Cru; they have gone swimming at Steps Beach; and Mitzi has even relaxed her no-red-meat rule and enjoyed a couple of Kelley's expertly grilled burgers.

But will Mitzi be okay with leaving the island for a vacation?

Kelley gives the planning everything he's got, both strategically and financially. He rents a Jaguar, the height of luxury (and fast, Kelley thinks). They will drive to Boston, have dinner at Alden and Harlow in Cambridge, and stay at the Langham, Mitzi's favorite hotel—then in the morning, after breakfast in bed, they'll drive to Deerfield, Massachusetts, and meander through the three-hundred-year-old village. From Deerfield, they'll head to Hanover, New Hampshire, to have lunch at Dartmouth (Mitzi's father, Joe, played basketball for Dartmouth in 1953 and Mitzi has always felt an affinity for the place), and then they'll drive to Stowe, Vermont, and stay at the Topnotch, a resort.

From Stowe, it's up to Vermont's Northeast Kingdom to spend the night in St. Johnsbury. From there, they'll go to Franconia Notch State Park, where they'll ride the Cannon Mountain Aerial Tramway for the ultimate in foliage viewing. They'll end with a night in charming Portsmouth, New Hampshire, a town Kelley thinks is possibly the best-kept secret in America. He has arranged for a couple's massage in front of the fire, for them to go apple-picking, on a hayride, out to dinners at fine country inns where bottles of champagne will be chilled and waiting on the tables, and for a personal yoga instructor in Stowe and then again in Portsmouth. He has made a mix of Mitzi's favorite songs to play on the drive, and he's packing up pumpkin muffins and his famous snack mix (secret ingredient: Bugles!) in case they get hungry on the road.

He prints out their itinerary on creamy paper and presents it to Mitzi one night before bed.

"Don't say anything until you've read it through," Kelley says. He fears Mitzi's knee-jerk reaction will be to say no, they can't go, what if they miss news about Bart, what if Bart comes home and neither of them is there? Irrational arguments born out of her very real pain.

Mitzi does as he asks and reads the itinerary. When she looks up at him, her eyes are shining with tears.

"You went through all this trouble for me?" she says.

"For us," he says.

"It looks wonderful," she says. "I can't wait."

JENNIFER

She goes to outpatient drug treatment at Patrick's insistence and although Jennifer protests initially, she also feels relieved—when caught red-handed by Patrick and Kevin in Norah's driveway, she had worried that Patrick would ship her off to Hazelden or Betty Ford. Jennifer had also been concerned about Norah. Were Patrick and Kevin going to call the police? Patrick told her not to worry about Norah, to worry only about herself and getting out of the grip of drugs.

Yes, okay. Jennifer has excelled at everything her entire life and she decides she's going to excel at rehab. She goes through the lectures and the therapy, but it's harder than anyone can imagine. Jennifer feels like her body hates her. She can't keep food down; she can't sleep; she can't wake up. She shakes, she sweats, she feels ugh, she feels ick.

Patrick is a champion at the beginning. He is the person Jennifer was when Patrick first went to prison—steadfast, supportive, kind. He checks in with her every few hours; he picks up the slack with the kids. But after a few weeks, he seems to believe the problem is solved, the war won. Jennifer is off drugs; her therapy decreases from every day to twice a week to once a week. She pees in a cup; she is pronounced clean.

Patrick is busy trying to get his hedge fund up and running. He has sixteen million dollars from investors, all of them people he has worked with in the past who continue to believe him capable of big things. He would like to double or triple that amount. It's not easy convincing new investors that he's legit, but he's persistent in presenting his business plan and a list of personal references. He's working out of his and Jennifer's home office, and he requires absolute silence; he seems resentful that Jennifer is also running a business out of that office—a successful business, she might add—and that she has fabric samples and Pantones lying around everywhere. Jennifer is basically forced to move her operation to the formal dining room— they never use it anyway, but she resents being ousted. Patrick yells at the children when they get home from school. He bans the PlayStation 4. Barrett and Pierce both complain to Jennifer. They start spending the afternoons at their friends' houses.

Jennifer says to Patrick, "You're alienating your own children."

Patrick gives her an incredulous look. "Do you or do you not want money? I have to start from scratch here. I'd like to build something quality, and that takes both time and concentration. I can't focus when the boys are stealing cars and killing zombies a floor above me, I'm sorry."

Jennifer's drug counselor, Sable, a lovely, refined woman in her midfifties, strongly encourages Jennifer to give up all mind-altering substances, including alcohol. But Jennifer can't, she simply *can't* give up her wine. "I'm not an alcoholic," she tells Sable.

Sable gives her a steady look. Sable has shared bits and pieces of her own history. When she was a slender young woman in her twenties, she worked for a drug dealer on the Canadian border. She kept guns under her bed and had a refrigerator full of money.

"They told me I would be okay as long as I didn't start using," Sable said. "And they were right. Once I started using, I sank like a stone."

Now, Sable says, "Alcohol impairs our judgment. My main fear is you drink, you get hooked back on pills."

"That won't happen," Jennifer assures her.

But one Friday night after a particularly trying week, Jennifer pours herself a second glass of wine, then a third, then a fourth. The boys are out at sleepovers and Jennifer has made veal chops with blue cheese mashed potatoes and a lavish spinach salad for herself and Patrick—but at eight o'clock, Patrick is still locked in "their" office, working.

After her fifth glass of wine, Jennifer pounds on the office door. Patrick opens it. He's on the phone but she doesn't care.

"Hang up!" she screams. "Hang! Up!"

What follows is the worst fight of their sixteen-year union. *Everything* comes out. Jennifer *hates* what Patrick did, hates the besmirching of their family name, hates that all the parents at the kids' schools look at her and the kids askance. People say they don't judge, but of course they *do* judge. They think Patrick is a cheater and a fraud and that Jennifer is guilty by association. Then it's Patrick's turn to retaliate: He can't believe Jennifer let herself fall prey to the allure of pharmaceuticals. *It's so predictable!* he says. He doesn't understand how she could lose control that way when she was *in charge of their children!*

"Don't you dare," Jennifer says. "Don't you dare imply that my parenting was in any way compromised."

"Wasn't it?" Patrick asks. "Be truthful with me. Be truthful with yourself. Did you ever drive the children while you were high?"

Jennifer fish-mouths. She wants to be indignant, wants to say she would never, ever have done such a thing—but she can't lie. There *were* some moments when she parented while high. She got lost driving home from one of Pierce's away lacrosse games and ended up in Revere. Revere, of all places! While on oxy, she lost her temper with Barrett, used some atrocious language, had an accident in the kitchen. While on Ativan, she fell asleep reading to Jaime more times than she could count, sometimes not even making it through a single page.

She starts to cry. "I failed you," she says.

"No," Patrick says. "I failed you. Your addiction to oxy and Ativan is my fault."

As much as Jennifer would like to hand Patrick the blame, she won't. "I'm an adult," she says. "Taking the pills was my decision. Seeking out more—from Norah—was my decision. A decision I made again and again."

They are no longer angry. Now, they are sad. Patrick opens his arms; Jennifer crawls into them. They make love, possibly the fiercest, most passionate love of their marriage, and Jennifer thinks that maybe, just maybe, everything is going to be all right.

Later, they eat the blue cheese mashed potatoes out of the pot while standing in front of the stove. Patrick gnaws on a veal chop while Jennifer attacks the spinach salad.

He says, "I don't want to ruin our beautiful détente, but we have to talk about my mother."

Jennifer closes her eyes. Margaret Quinn is now Jennifer's least favorite subject. Jennifer has over a dozen voicemail messages from Margaret, but she hasn't been able to listen to a single one.

"You can't avoid her forever," Patrick says. "She's my mother. She's the boys' grandmother."

"I know," Jennifer whispers.

"She doesn't think any less of you," Patrick says. "She isn't like that."

Jennifer spears a cherry tomato, then a slice of white button mushroom. There's no way to make Patrick understand how mortified Jennifer is that Margaret knows about her addiction. Telling her own mother and Mitzi and Kelley wasn't great, but it was better than admitting her addiction to Margaret Quinn. The shame of what she's done and how she's done it has frozen the previously wonderful relationship Jennifer had with her mother-in-law. Jennifer can't bring herself to call Margaret back, and texting feels like a cop-out. She has considered writing Margaret a letter but she doesn't know what she would say.

Margaret doesn't think any less of Jennifer—that's a bold-faced lie. Of course Margaret thinks less of her! Jennifer has striven for perfection in every aspect and especially in every aspect Margaret can see. Jennifer has never valued anyone's opinion or sought anyone's approval as much as Margaret's. But now, Jennifer has blown it. She has disgraced herself and proven herself unworthy.

Margaret isn't like that—true, she isn't like that. She was very restrained in expressing her disappointment with Patrick. She couldn't have liked the situation but she remained supportive and nonjudgmental. Jennifer realizes Margaret will probably be understanding—Jennifer was dealing with a lot, her circumstances made her vulnerable—but in her most honest, most secret and forever thoughts, Margaret will see Jennifer as weak.

"I can't call her," Jennifer says. "I just can't."

"Every day you wait makes it worse," Patrick says. "Call her right now. Get it over with."

"I can't," Jennifer says. "I've been drinking."

Patrick nods. "In the morning, then."

"Okay?" Jennifer says. She sets down her fork. She has lost her appetite.

In the morning, Jennifer and Patrick make love again and Jennifer hopes the act is distracting enough that Patrick will forget about Jennifer calling Margaret. But only seconds before he steps into the shower, he turns to Jennifer, who is at the sink brushing her teeth, and says, "My mother. Do it now. You promised."

She knows for a fact that she *didn't* promise; she knows

she said *Okay?* with a question mark in her voice. She had said *Okay?* only to put the topic to bed. Was he really going to hold her to her *Okay?*

She nods, spits, shuts off the water, and leaves the bathroom.

She sits on her bed holding her cell phone. She has never dreaded anything in her life as much as she dreads dialing Margaret's number. But putting it off means having it hang over her head, which is stressful enough to make Jennifer crave an Ativan.

Vicious cycle. She will not fall prey to it.

She dials the number, brings the phone to her ear. It's nine o'clock on a Saturday morning so Margaret won't be working, but she may still be asleep, or at the gym, or making Drake an omelet.

"Hello?" Margaret says, sounding fresh and awake.

"Margaret?" Jennifer says. Her heart is slamming in her chest. "It's Jennifer."

"Jennifer?" Margaret says. She sounds confused, and Jennifer realizes Margaret doesn't recognize her voice. Margaret must know five hundred Jennifers, including Lopez, Lawrence, and Aniston.

"Your daughter-in-law," Jennifer says. She squeezes her eyes shut.

"Jennifer!" Margaret says. "You must think me monstrous. Drake tells me I shouldn't answer my phone without checking the caller ID, but I can never find my glasses. And I'm supposed to be interviewing a woman named Jennifer to be my new assistant. I thought maybe you were her."

"New assistant?" Jennifer says. "What's happening to Darcy?"

"Darcy will be leaving in a month or so," Margaret says. "CNN is making her a full producer. She's moving to Atlanta. Isn't that the most awful thing you've ever heard?"

"Yes," Jennifer says. "Darcy is . . . she is . . ."

"My right hand," Margaret says. "I don't know about this other Jennifer. She graduated summa cum laude from Princeton and she sounds very tightly wound. How are you, my darling?"

"Oh," Jennifer says, her breath coming more easily now. "I'm okay, I guess."

"Well, there's something I wanted to talk to you about," Margaret says.

Here it comes, Jennifer thinks. The inevitable lecture. The scolding. The description of Margaret's disappointment. Or, worse, a bestowal of forgiveness. If Margaret says something kind, or if she says that each and every one of us is human and therefore susceptible to the occasional failure and it doesn't make us bad people, Jennifer will cry. She doesn't deserve to be the recipient of Margaret's generous understanding.

"Margaret . . ." Jennifer says. She feels she should pre-empt Margaret with an apology, but Margaret doesn't give her a chance.

"I want to throw Isabelle a bridal shower, but I don't have time to plan it," Margaret says. "Will you help me? Please? You have the most exquisite taste."

"I do?" Jennifer says. "I mean, of course I'll help. I can plan the whole thing, if you'd like." She can't believe that Margaret is treating her like a person instead of an addict. The pills didn't define her, Jennifer realizes then. Tears come, but they are tears of relief, not sadness, and Jennifer wipes them away.

"That would be such a help," Margaret says. "Thank you, thank you, darling girl. You're the best."

AVA

Most people make their resolutions in January, but Ava decided to do it on the first day of school and now, nearly two months in, she has stuck to them quite admirably.

1. Learn to be happy alone.
2. No men.

The second resolution was put there to reinforce the meaning of the first. In order for Ava to be happy alone, she can't have a boyfriend, and she can't date. She refuses Nathaniel's repeated invitations to visit him on Block Island. *You'll love it,* he says. It's like Nantucket, he says, except smaller—only ten square miles—and simpler. There are only 108 children in the school district, and everyone in the seventh grade has to play in the band.

"Isn't that great?" Nathaniel says.

Ava is sure it's charming, but she doesn't want anything simpler than Nantucket. Recently, she's been having city dreams.

Every once in a while, she'll get a text from Potter that says, *NYC this weekend?* It's tempting, but...Ava wants to stick to her resolutions.

As she tells Shelby, "I've been in a relationship with either Nathaniel or Scott for the past three and a half years."

"Before that, you dated Ben, the visiting art teacher," Shelby says.

"Oh, that's right," Ava says. Ben the visiting art teacher was a real character with his beret and his goatee. He knew about matcha before it was a thing. Mitzi had *loved* Ben the visiting art teacher; that in itself spoke volumes. Before Ben, there was Moose, a bouncer at the Bar. Moose was six foot six, a man of very few words and of very simple tastes. That relationship had lasted only four months, just long enough for the novelty of his size to wear off. "It's even worse than I thought. I haven't been single in six years. I can't remember who I used to be," Ava says now.

"I bet you can't make it to Christmas without getting back into a relationship," Shelby says.

"I'll take that bet," Ava says with a bravado she does not feel. "Shall we say dinner at the Club Car? With caviar?"

"You're on," Shelby says.

Avoiding Nathaniel and Potter is one thing—they live elsewhere. But avoiding Scott is quite another matter. Ava has to see him every single day. She keeps the interaction to a nod of the head; if she has any administrative questions, she goes directly to Principal Kubisch.

Ava is amazed at how much leisure time she has without a boyfriend. She has her mountain bike serviced and goes on long, elaborate rides for her autumn Saturdays— up to Altar Rock and over to Jewel Pond, through the state forest to Nobadeer Beach. On weekend nights, she goes to Shelby and Zack's house, where Zack makes braised short ribs or truffled mac and cheese and they drink red wine and tell stories about the students until they're in stitches. Or Ava stays home with Kelley and Mitzi; they order Thai food and binge on *Ray Donovan,* and then always, before bed, they sit in Bart's bedroom for a few minutes. The light is always kept on in that room as they wait for his return. Then Kelley and Mitzi retire to their bedroom. Ava has noticed how much older Kelley looks since his illness, and he has slowed way down. Mitzi looks older too, but in a more settled and relaxed way. She is more approachable than she has ever been, so approachable that one morning over coffee, Ava says, "How are you feeling about Bart?"

Ava would never have dared ask this question before; Mitzi was far too volatile, the shock and pain of Bart's disappearance too raw, her psyche too fragile.

Mitzi shakes her head. "I know I should fall further into despair with each day that passes, every day there's no news. That was what happened last year, when I was with George, and it nearly ruined me. I work very hard on my positive visualization and my faith. In my bones, in my *gut,* I feel that Bart is alive. That boy, Private Burke, when he regains his faculties is going to give the military the information they need."

Ava would like to believe this. Private William Burke is conscious and making great strides every day, but he suffers from amnesia. Amnesia—Ava thought this was a fictional condition used as a plot device in the movies. But apparently, it's real. Private Burke has no memory of the events that brought him to the hospital. He remembers landing in Afghanistan and climbing aboard the convoy. That's it; the rest is a blank. The doctors aren't sure if the memory loss was caused by the head trauma he sustained or by the things he experienced while in captivity; perhaps they were so grisly that his mind erased them as a defense mechanism. He sees therapists every day. Ava imagines these counselors as locksmiths trying to insert the key that will free his memory.

"Plus," Mitzi says, "the DoD is still searching, every day. Eventually, they're going to find those boys. They're going to find Bart."

Find Bart. Now that Ava is finished with men, she has more time to dedicate to thinking about Bart.

One afternoon following her bike ride, she slips into the

five o'clock Mass at St. Mary's. She's wearing her yoga pants and sneakers and so she sits in the last row, hoping God will be happy she actually attended church of her own accord and so will forgive her attire. (When Ava was growing up, Margaret had two steadfast rules for church: no jeans and no eating an hour before Mass.)

She prays for Bart. She prays for Mitzi and Kelley. She begs for forgiveness; she has been so absorbed with the drama of her romantic life that she has, at times, forgotten that her brother is missing, ignored the fact that he is, most likely, suffering. He's cold, he's starving, he'd dehydrated, he's emaciated, he's being beaten or tortured, he's worried about all of them worrying about him.

Bart!

Ava lights a candle after Mass. She imagines the flame warming Bart, igniting hope inside him. *We will find you,* she thinks. *You will be returned to us.* Mitzi practices positive visualization. She has done this as long as Ava has known her. Mitzi used to visualize parking spots in town; she visualized Patrick getting accepted to Colgate; she visualized Norah deciding to have her python tattoo removed. Sometimes her visualizations worked, sometimes they didn't.

But why not give it a shot?

Ava visualizes a Special Forces team rescuing Bart. She sees him staggering forward and falling into the soldiers' arms. He will be exhausted and hungry and injured. He will shed his first tears since he's been captured.

And then, the trip home. From Afghanistan to Germany to New York; from New York to Boston; from Boston to Nantucket. Ava pictures her brother wearily climbing the front steps of the inn, opening the door, and flinging his rucksack down.

It's me—Bart, he will say. *I'm home.*

*   *   *

The first week in November, Ava is due to have her second-grade class observed, and the person who does classroom observations and evaluations is…Scott. There is no way around this. Ava is going to have to endure forty minutes with Scott Skyler sitting in the back of the class with his clipboard.

Last year, Scott observed Ava with her most obnoxious class of fifth-graders. Ava had complained about this particular class all year long—all of the teachers had—but with Mr. Skyler in the back of the class, every student had behaved. Even Topher Fotea; even Ryan Papsycki. Ava remembered feeling in awe of the influence Scott had with the kids. He had power. He had always been Ava's hero, but during that class, he had been a superhero.

She will not allow herself to feel that way this year. This year, she will teach an inspired lesson about keeping a beat, using wood blocks to demonstrate. She will pretend Scott doesn't exist.

This is easier said than done. Scott enters the classroom and the second-graders—a darling, sweet group—all gather around him, clamoring for his attention, especially the little girls. Ava suffers an unfortunate image of Scott as the father of all of these children, the kind of magnetic, involved father that every child dreams of. She notices that he's wearing the blue-checked shirt she bought him for his birthday, and his Vineyard Vines tie printed with cartoon images of fish tacos. Did he wear that shirt and tie on purpose? Of course he did.

The more pressing problem is that as soon as he sets foot in the music room, the air smells like him. Scott always smells deliciously of this certain maple soap that his mother sends him from Vermont. The scent is sweetly reminiscent of pancakes but also contains a tang of evergreen. It's distracting. Ava claps her hands and asks the second-graders to please use their indoor voices and take their seats.

"Mr. Skyler is here to see if you're better behaved than Ms. Colby's class."

"We are!" they say, and they sit and zip their lips, as Ava has taught them.

After Ava escorts the second-graders back to their classroom, she is to meet with Scott to go over the highs and lows of the lesson. This is the part Ava is really dreading—thirty minutes alone with Scott in her room, the door closed to preserve the confidentiality of his evaluation.

She enters the room and gives him a tight smile. She is wearing a black turtleneck, a black-and-white giraffe-print skirt, and high black suede boots. Since she gave up men and started riding her bike so much, she has lost twelve pounds.

"You look great, Ava," Scott says. "I can't get over how great."

"Is that part of my evaluation?" Ava asks. "The Massachusetts Board of Education wants to know how I look?"

"Ava..."

"Please," Ava says. "Don't be unprofessional."

Scott nods once, sharply, then proceeds to go over his notes. He has given her a five out of five in every category, and as an anecdotal, he has written: *Ms. Quinn continues to offer her students a strong and engaging education in music by using innovative, hands-on lesson plans that not only teach students the basic elements of composition but allow them to make music themselves. Ms. Quinn's classroom management is superlative. Her students respect her; they listen and obey classroom rules. I have no suggestions for improvement. Ms. Quinn would be well advised to, in the words of Bob Dylan, "keep on keepin' on." Her skills are obvious; her demeanor admirable. She is a credit to our school and sets a high bar for instruction.*

Ava blinks. Is he expressing his honest opinion or just kissing her ass? She doesn't care. The evaluation is glowing; Ava is free from this torture for another year.

"Okay," she says. "Thank you."

"Ava..."

The bell rings. It's her lunch period. Tuesday means tuna salad on wheat and clam chowder. The culinary class up at the high school makes the chowder from scratch, and it's some of the best on the island.

"I have to go," she says.

"Just give me five minutes," he says. "There are some things I want to say."

Ava doesn't want to hear the things Scott Skyler has to say, but his brown eyes are searching hers in such an earnest way that she doesn't have the heart to walk away.

"Speak," she says.

"Ava, I love you," he says.

She scoffs. "Last Christmas Stroll, you took Roxanne to the hospital on a Good Samaritan mission and you never returned to me. Not really. You skipped the Festival of Trees; you missed Genevieve's baptism. And then you started dating Roxanne."

"You were with Nathaniel," Scott says.

"You never should have gone with Roxanne to the hospital," Ava says. "If you had stayed with me on Nantucket, we would be engaged by now."

"Yes," he whispers.

"But we're not."

"Roxanne needed me," Scott says.

"No," Ava says. "Roxanne wanted you. Despite the fact that you were *my* boyfriend. She set her sights on you and you were hers. Women who look like Roxanne Oliveria always get what they want."

"It wasn't how she looked..." Scott says.

"Scott," Ava says. "Come on."

"Okay," Scott says and he raises his palms. Ava has always been a sucker for Scott's hands—broad, strong, capable. She looks down at her desk, where the sheet music for "Annie's Song" rests. Next week, the fourth-graders receive their recorders and they will begin practicing for graduation. It's a never-ending cycle of *You fill up my senses.* "I thought Roxanne was beautiful, yes, I did. I thought, quite frankly, that she was out of my league. Most women are."

"But, apparently, not me," Ava says. She gives a dry, disgusted laugh. "Thanks."

"Roxanne is beautiful only on the outside," Scott says. "Inside, she's needy and narcissistic, flaky and irritating."

"I can't believe you're saying those things about the almost mother of your child."

Scott winces. "She hasn't been the same since the miscarriage."

"My understanding is that few women are the same," Ava says.

"She's really messed up," Scott says. "She goes to a therapist every day. I went the first few times but then I had to stop."

"Are you two still seeing each other? At all?" Ava hates asking, but she has to know.

"Not really," he says.

What a wimpy answer! Ava stands up. Her chowder is calling.

"Ava," he says, "I was just as shocked as you were when Roxanne got pregnant. I was...well, my first response wasn't joy, I can tell you that."

"But you've always wanted to be a father," Ava says. She feels herself reaching an emotional edge. Roxanne had given Scott his dream.

He takes both of Ava's hands. This is *not okay*, but his grip is so firm, she can't pull away.

"I wanted to be the father of *your* children," he says. "I love *you*. I never loved Roxanne. I got caught in her web somehow. And then you were with Nathaniel, and a part of me believed you had always wanted to be with Nathaniel…"

"Don't make this my fault," Ava says. "I didn't let Nathaniel get me pregnant."

"He proposed," Scott says. "You accepted."

"You were in Tuscany with Roxanne!" Ava says.

"What does that have to do with anything?" Scott says.

They are both on their feet now, glaring at each other over Ava's desk. It's a standoff.

Scott capitulates. "I love you, Ava. I want to be with you now. I want to be with you forever."

These are words that Ava would have relished at another time, but at the moment, they feel a day late and a dollar short. She loves Scott too; that isn't the problem. The problem is that he was going to have a baby with Roxanne Oliveria. He was going to be connected with her in an everlasting, irrevocable way, and that had been okay with him. He had bidden Ava good-bye. He had used the term *cold turkey*.

"I haven't told anyone this," Ava says.

Scott's brown eyes open a little wider. Ava tries to ignore the thick brown hair that she used to grab in moments of passion.

"This is my last year at Nantucket Elementary," Ava says.

"What?" Scott says.

"Yep," Ava says. "I'm moving to New York. Next September, I'm teaching there."

Scott seems to be at a loss. "What?"

"I'm done living at the inn," Ava says. "I want to grow up. I want to be a person. My own person."

"Ava..." Scott says.

"Consider this my notice," Ava says.

KEVIN

Kevin Quinn is the king of the world. At the selectmen's meeting on Wednesday, November 9, Kevin is granted a three-year liquor license for his venue, Quinns' on the Beach, at 200 Surfside Road. The total cost, with all of the permitting fees and insurance, is just under a hundred and twenty grand. Kevin figures he will easily make this money back in the first year. Kevin did note that his most vocal champion among the selectmen was none other than Chester Silva, Haven's uncle, who said he liked to see "local kids" running successful island businesses. Kevin smiles at the word *kid*. He's thirty-eight years old. But Chester is in his seventies, so he supposes it's all relative.

That accomplished, Kevin finds a small, year-round rental on the edge of town. It's just a cottage, two bedrooms, two baths—but it's charming and warm. There is a cozy downstairs bedroom for Genevieve, and an airy, spacious loft-type master suite for Kevin and Isabelle. There are granite countertops in the kitchen and a breakfast nook, a clawfoot tub in Genevieve's bathroom, and a postage-stamp-size yard where, come spring, Genevieve can toddle around.

Once Kevin and Isabelle have moved in—man, does it feel good to have their own space!—Kevin focuses all his energy on the wedding. He has purchased plane tickets for Arnaud and Helene, Isabelle's parents, who will arrive on December 23 and stay for four nights in room 10 at the inn—George's old room. The ceremony will be held at the Siasconset Union Chapel at three o'clock in the afternoon. Kevin can't begin to explain the hoops he had to jump through to make this happen in the off-season— even with space heaters, the chapel will be chilly—but St. Mary's is busy with Christmas Eve services, and Isabelle is adamant about a church wedding. Kevin has asked Father Paul, the priest the Quinn family grew up with, to return to Nantucket from the mainland to perform the ceremony. The "reception" will be the annual Winter Street Inn Christmas party, only this year the party will be catered because Isabelle isn't to lift a finger.

Mitzi and Kelley have been very supportive of these plans. The only hiccup came when Kevin brought up the topic of groomsmen. He had initially thought he would be attended by Patrick as best man and Pierre, his boss from the Bar, as the other groomsman, while Isabelle would have Ava and Jennifer.

"But what about Bart?" Mitzi had asked.

Kevin had stared at her, not quite understanding the question.

She said, "He'll be hurt if you don't make him a groomsman."

Kevin nodded slowly. Bart would most definitely want to be a groomsman—if he weren't being held prisoner in Afghanistan. But Kevin quickly realized that Mitzi's hopes ran high and if Kevin wanted her full cooperation, he would have to get with the program and proceed as if Bart would be back on Nantucket by December 24.

"Bart will be my groomsman," Kevin said. "I'll just have Pierre as backup."

"You won't need a backup," Mitzi said. "Why don't you ask Pierre to be a reader?"

"Okay," Kevin said. "That's what I'll do."

JENNIFER

Jennifer throws Isabelle's bridal shower the weekend before Thanksgiving. Her primary stumbling block is that Isabelle has few friends on the island so there aren't enough attendees for a full-blown party. She decides to reserve the elegant red dining room upstairs at Le Languedoc. Isabelle will feel comfortable and cozy. There will be French champagne and French bistro food. Jennifer invites Margaret, Mitzi, Ava, Ava's best friend, Shelby, and then, truly desperate for warm bodies, she asks Mary Rose Garth, George's girlfriend. Everyone accepts; both Margaret and Mitzi are thrilled, Kevin is grateful, and Jennifer feels more like herself than she has since the day Patrick was indicted. She is helping out, getting things done. Isabelle will have a proper bridal shower in an elegant French restaurant.

Patrick and Jennifer arrive on Nantucket for the shower on Saturday afternoon. The streets of town feel deserted because many locals are on Martha's Vineyard for the annual high school football game known as the Island Cup. Jennifer bought Isabelle a set of plush white towels monogrammed with her and Kevin's initials, but once Jennifer's on the island, she goes to Ladybird Lingerie on Centre Street because she wants to get Isabelle something pretty to wear on her honeymoon.

As Jennifer is heading back to the inn with the gift, she sees a black truck rumbling down the cobblestones of Main Street. Jennifer's heart seizes.

It's Norah's truck.

The truck stops abruptly, the driver's window goes down, and Norah sticks her head out. "Hey, you."

She sounds normal, friendly, and she looks wonderful. She has gotten her hair colored and styled by someone who knows what he or she is doing, and Norah looks at once younger and more sophisticated.

Drugs, Jennifer thinks. *Oxy, Ativan.* A familiar longing stirs in her.

"Hey," Jennifer says. She isn't sure whether to stop and chat or hurry along up the sidewalk. To stop might make for an uncomfortable situation, but to speed up might seem rude. Jennifer compromises by slowing down somewhat.

Norah nods at Jennifer's shopping bag from Ladybird. "Get a little something to surprise Paddy?"

"Oh," Jennifer says. "This is for Isabelle."

"Kev's girl?" Norah asks.

Jennifer presses her lips together. She finds herself unable to lie to Norah—but why not?

"Are they getting married?" Norah asks. "Finally?"

Jennifer smiles and keeps walking.

"I'll take that as a yes," Norah says. "Good for Kev. He deserves to be happy."

"Yes," Jennifer says, perhaps more forcefully than she intends. "He does."

"When is the wedding?" Norah asks.

Jennifer will not tell her. She waves and picks up her pace.

"Okay, then," Norah says. She drives away.

The shower is sheer perfection, if Jennifer does say so herself. The seven women gather in the vestibule of the restaurant, and everyone is in high spirits, especially Isabelle. She is smiling more brightly than Jennifer has ever seen her smile. Isabelle isn't a woman who is used to being celebrated, a fact that breaks Jennifer's heart a little but also makes her happy that Isabelle is marrying Kevin.

Jimmy, the bartender at Le Languedoc and a friend of the Quinn family for many years, leads the women upstairs. The stairs are narrow and steep in a way that promises an *arrival*—and the room does not disappoint. It is hushed and elegant, the table exquisitely set with white linen, silver, china, crystal, and a low, wide bouquet of fall flowers, a gift from Kevin. There is a magnum of Veuve Clicquot chilling in an ice bucket. At everyone's place sit two gifts: a wrapped copy of Elin Hilderbrand's wedding-on-Nantucket novel, *Beautiful Day* (Isabelle's copy is in French, and obtaining it took a bit of logistical gymnastics on Jennifer's part), and a small blue box from Tiffany, tied up with white satin ribbon.

Mary Rose gushes as she takes her seat, marked by a calligraphed place card. "I've never been to a shower where *I* got a present," she says.

Margaret squeezes Jennifer's arm. "You did a beautiful job, sweetie," she says. "You went above and beyond."

That was by design: Jennifer had badly wanted to impress Margaret and restore herself in her mother-in-law's good graces. Plus, staging moments like this was Jennifer's job. She had built a career on making her clients' homes gracious and comfortable, practical yet inspiring. Essentially, she created set decorations to encourage happy, productive, peaceful lives. But what actually happened in the rooms Jennifer curated was, of course, beyond her control.

Inside each Tiffany box was a heart-shaped silver bookmark engraved with the guest's initials.

"Inspired!" Ava says. She grins at Jennifer. "I'm never getting married, but if I do, I want you to plan my shower."

It is one of the most convivial and relaxed evenings Jennifer has had in a long, long time. The service at Le Languedoc is seamless, the food sublime. Isabelle is thrilled with the escargot and the steak-frites. Jennifer orders the chopped salad and the pan-roasted lobster over soft polenta, which she can't finish and so decides to take it home for Patrick. He'll be thrilled. They drink one magnum of champagne and order a second. Jennifer had worried about the triumvirate of Margaret, Mitzi, and Mary Rose, but the three of them chat away like sorority sisters. Mitzi is in surprisingly good spirits, considering Thanksgiving is only a week away and Bart still isn't home. Mary Rose fits into the group easily; they might as well start calling her Aunt Mary Rose.

Before dessert is served—Jennifer requested an opera cake, Isabelle's favorite—Margaret taps her glass with her spoon then stands to make a toast.

"When my children were growing up," she says, "I used to joke that I spent five percent of my time taking care of Patrick, five percent of my time taking care of Ava, and ninety percent of my time taking care of Kevin."

The table chuckles. Jennifer has heard all the stories about Kevin as a kid—the poor grades, the detentions, the scrambling for missing homework and forgotten lunches. Now that Jennifer is the mother of three, she sees that Kevin has long been a victim of birth order, stuck behind

Patrick, who is good at everything and driven to do better, and Ava, the baby and only daughter. When Jennifer first met Kevin, she thought he was cute and sweet, a laid-back, less serious version of Patrick, and something about him had appealed to her. Of course, back then Kevin had been defined—absolutely *defined*—by Norah Vale. Norah had been a black sorceress, leading Kevin down a path of darkness. Kevin had been both afraid of Norah and dependent on her.

Sort of like Jennifer herself had been. Oh boy.

"Of my three children, Kevin has taken the longest to figure out who he wants to be. I'm not going to lie... Kelley and I were worried about him."

More chuckles. Mitzi raises her hand. "And me."

"And Mitzi," Margaret says. She turns to Isabelle, her green eyes shining. "Kevin's dreams started coming true once he found the right person to share them with. Look at how he has thrived and grown since he met you, Isabelle. He's become a father. He's started his own business. And he has a home—finally. So it is from all of Kevin's concerned parents that I raise my glass to you, Isabelle, and say, *Merci beaucoup.*"

"To Isabelle," Ava says.

They clink glasses.

Isabelle opens her gifts while they enjoy the opera cake: the towels and tasteful lingerie from Jennifer, some less tasteful lingerie from Mary Rose—which gets the table hooting—a gift certificate to the RJ Miller salon from Shelby, some scented candles and a gift certificate for ten yoga sessions from Mitzi, a gorgeous silver picture frame from Ava, and a pair of Ted Muehling earrings from Margaret. Jennifer has wisely brought a couple of empty shopping bags so that Isabelle can get her haul home.

They leave the restaurant and head out into the frosty autumn air. Isabelle catches up with Jennifer on the street and gives her a hug. Jennifer recognizes that this is a big deal—Isabelle is very reserved and private and she is *not* touchy-feely in the slightest.

"Merci beaucoup à toi, ma soeur," Isabelle says. "Thank you with all my heart."

"Oh, Isabelle, you're welcome," Jennifer says, closing her eyes. She's filled with a warm syrupy feeling that's a combination of pride and accomplishment and love. But then Jennifer opens her eyes and sees the black truck parked across the street.

It can't be.

Is it?

Jennifer freezes. Norah Vale waves.

MARGARET

Margaret had hoped her frenetic schedule might calm down a bit after the election, but the short week before Thanksgiving is jam-packed with activity. Margaret and Ava leave Nantucket together the day after Isabelle's bridal shower and head back to the city. Ava has interviews at four Manhattan private schools, three on Monday and one on Tuesday.

Ava, it seems, is moving to the city.

Margaret will not let herself get too excited, although it's difficult. A piece of her has yearned for Ava's daily presence since Kelley moved the three kids up to Nantucket twenty years earlier. Now, the joy of possibly having her daughter in the city on a permanent basis crowds out all other thoughts. It becomes all Margaret wants, and she has to keep herself from offering Ava the moon: She will buy Ava her own apartment! She will hire Ava a driver! She will pay Ava's gym membership at Equinox. She and Ava will go to the theater every week and brunch at Le Bilboquet every Sunday. Margaret thinks back to when Paddy and Kevin were small and Ava just a baby and how *drained* she had felt, how shackled. All she had wished for was freedom to pursue her career. Then, when she did pursue her career, she was encumbered with debilitating guilt. It was the challenge of working mothers everywhere, she supposed: wanting to be in two places at once. Margaret had struggled to raise her children while still nurturing herself. Back then, Margaret could never have guessed that, when she was sixty-one, the people she would most want to spend time with—aside from Drake—would be her grown children.

Ava moving to the city is too much to hope for. It's like an iridescent soap bubble—if Margaret touches it, it will pop. Ava may get to the city and find it noisy and overwhelming, chaotic and dirty, and run back to the safe, close-knit community of Nantucket, where she is a big fish in a small pond. Manhattan can be an intimidating place even when every door is open.

Margaret kisses Ava good-bye on Monday morning. Ava is wearing a blue-and-white DVF wrap dress and a pair of nude Manolo heels, both borrowed from Margaret. She looks beautiful and professional.

"Are you *sure* you don't want Raoul to take you around?" Margaret asks. "He's happy to do it. He'll welcome the change."

"I'm sure," Ava says. "I can walk, and if it starts to rain, I'll take a taxi."

"Okay," Margaret says. "We'll see you at eight o'clock tonight at Café Cluny."

"West Twelfth Street," Ava says.

"Yes," Margaret says. She picked that restaurant because it's close to Drake's apartment, and the plan is—if Ava moves to the city—she will live in Drake's apartment until she saves enough money to get a place of her own. "But downtown can be confusing. If you want, you can meet me at the studio."

"Mom," Ava says. "Stop worrying about me. I'll be fine."

Ava looks better than fine at eight o'clock at Café Cluny. She is already seated when Drake and Margaret arrive. She has changed into jeans, boots, a shimmery top, and a suede fringed jacket.

"How did it go?" Margaret asks. Her heart is in her throat, and Drake squeezes her hand, which is probably a signal that she should moderate her tone. He knows how badly she wants this.

"It was amazing," Ava says. "I already have verbal offers from two of the three schools."

Yes! Margaret barely stifles a cheer.

Drake says, "This calls for a toast."

AVA

She has never been one for princess fantasies, but her first day seeking a new life in New York makes her feel like Cinderella. She goes to interviews at three private schools, schools that might seem elitist to an outsider, but once Ava steps inside the hushed, rarefied atmosphere of learning, she is instantly converted. The commitment to music education and appreciation at all three schools is what Ava has dreamed of. At the first school, the Albany, there is a piano tuner kept *on staff.* Each of the three music conservatories contains a Steinway baby grand; there is live piano music for every level of ballet class. Ava is invited to sit down at one, and she can't help showing off, playing the same Schubert impromptu that she played when she was trying to impress Nathaniel. At the second school, Bainbridge Academy, attendance at one full season of the New York Philharmonic is required for graduation. And at the final school, Copper Hill, which is more progressive, there is a bona fide recording studio where students can write and produce their own original songs.

The headmasters at all three schools seem captivated by Ava and she wonders if they know she's Margaret Quinn's daughter. If so, they don't mention it. They are far too discreet and sophisticated, and in this stratum of New York, everyone rubs elbows with the famous all the time. Sophia Loren's granddaughter goes to the Albany, and Bainbridge Academy has the children of Broadway stars, bestselling novelists, and two starting linemen for the New York Giants. The headmasters seem intrigued by Ava's teaching career on Nantucket. It's such a small district, so far out to sea. *What is it like?* they ask. *Aren't you isolated?* Ava starts to feel as though she's been teaching in Never-Never Land and has only now decided to join the real world.

Her observation notes are excellent, the headmaster at the Albany tells her. Her recommendations are positively glowing. The Albany would like to hire her. The same is true at Bainbridge Academy—and the salaries at both schools are considerably higher than what she presently makes. At Copper Hill, where Ava would be overseeing the entire music department—including band, orchestra, choir, two madrigal groups, two a cappella groups, and the musical theater program—the process is longer and more involved. The headmistress at Copper Hill says she would like Ava to come back the next day to meet with the selection committee.

Ava has an interview scheduled at the Raleigh-Dawes School on the East Side at ten o'clock the next morning but after her last interview today, she decides to cancel. She wants the job at Copper Hill more than she has ever wanted anything in her life. It's a huge, challenging position where she would run a department, manage a budget, and encourage a philosophy of living a life steeped in the arts! It is so much bigger than her classroom job at Nantucket Elementary School that she feels intimidated. But also energized! This is a career. A career for Ava Quinn!

She expresses her fervent wish to her mother and Drake over dinner at Café Cluny.

"Copper Hill?" Margaret says. "On West Seventieth?"

Ava nods as she dives into her Cluny burger. This place is adorable and the food is delicious, and Ava is pretty sure Darcy picked it out when Margaret told her she needed somewhere that would make Ava feel excited about moving to New York. It does boggle Ava's mind how great this restaurant is, but there are thirty others just as good in a ten-block radius. The variety! The choices! Ava can't believe how long it's taken for her to realize what she's been missing.

"Lee and Ginny Kramer's children go to Copper Hill," Margaret says. "I'm sorry, I heard you say the names of the schools but I didn't put two and two together until just this second."

"Oh," Drake says, raising his eyebrows. "Does Lee sit on the board?"

Margaret laughs. "He hardly has time. And Ginny is even busier than Lee is. But..."

"No," Ava says. "Don't." She doesn't want any help from the head of CBS and the editor of *Vogue,* although a phone call from either one would no doubt do the trick. "I want to get this job on my own merits."

Drake plucks a frite from Margaret's plate. "Good for you," he says.

On the way to her second Copper Hill interview in the morning, Ava stops at Holy Trinity and lights a candle for Bart. *Is any act truly selfless?* she wonders. She aches for Bart's return as keenly as she ever has, but now there's even more at stake. She's likely going to leave Nantucket. Move out of the inn. Kelley and Mitzi will have an empty nest and Ava isn't sure they can handle that.

Ava is wearing a winter-white dress with black trim and black lace Manolo Blahniks—both her mother's. She loves dressing up for work and never gets the chance; she would sooner wear roller skates to Nantucket Elementary than heels. The only teacher in the district who wears heels is... Roxanne Oliveria.

Ava can't think about Roxanne right now. Here she goes!

She knocks the interview out of the park. She pauses and considers before every answer; she is funny, self-effacing, knowledgeable. She draws on her classical training at Peabody, her love of the piano, her practical experience with musical theater. (She directed *The King and I, Pippin*, and *Chitty Chitty Bang Bang* at the high school.) She sings a few bars from *Godspell.* Why not? And when they ask if she has anything to add, she says: "My father moved us from Manhattan to Nantucket when I was nine years old. My mother stayed in New York to pursue her career." Pause. She nearly said *her career in broadcasting* but then thought better of it. "My father wanted to raise us in a small, close-knit community where we didn't have to lock our cars, where we knew our neighbors, where we could ride our bikes to school. I love those aspects of Nantucket and I also love the way the island expands socially and intellectually in the summer. But I'm ready to grow beyond the confines of Nantucket. On a personal level, I am unencumbered—no husband, no children—so there is nothing and no one to stop me from getting some air under these wings. I am so excited by the opportunity to lead the music department at Copper Hill. You may have candidates who are more qualified, but you don't have anyone who will give this position more of him- or herself than me."

The committee looks—intrigued? Impressed? Ava mists up, then reins in her surging emotions.

The headmistress beams at her. "Thank you, Ava," she says. "We value nothing at Copper Hill more than heart."

Ava is all dialed up when she leaves the school. She wants to call her mother but Margaret is filming a *60 Minutes* interview with Ellen DeGeneres. Ava doesn't feel she can call her father, Mitzi, Kevin, or anyone on Nantucket; she fears they won't understand her brand-new love affair with the city. Shelby will be at school, and even if she took Ava's call, she would be the worst of the lot. Every time the topic of Ava moving to New York comes up, Shelby starts to cry.

Nathaniel? No.

Scott? Definitely not.

Who does she know who will appreciate her imminent leap into a new, urban life?

*   *   *

Potter Lyons is so excited to hear from Ava that Ava gets excited as well.

"I have a seminar from one to four today," he says. "Otherwise, I would take you out drinking. I can't believe you're *here!* I can't believe you're *moving* here!"

"Definitely moving," Ava says. She has the offers from the Albany and Bainbridge Academy, like two gold coins in her pocket. "The question is . . . great job or *dream* job?"

"Copper Hill is such a utopia," Potter says. "If the chairmanship of the literature department became available, I would snap it up."

"You'd leave the Ivy League?" Ava says.

"The students are ruined by the time they get to me," Potter says. "I love the wonder of high school kids. Middle school, even better. You can actually mold them, influence them, make a difference."

He's speaking her language. That's what Ava wants. A classroom filled with kids who want to learn.

"You have to have dinner with me tonight," Potter says. "Can you? There's a place called Fish down on Bleecker. It's basically a dive with cold PBR and a ridiculous raw bar. A guy shucks ten kinds of oysters while you throw peanut shells on the floor."

"Sounds divine," Ava says. Margaret and Drake have a benefit for the Boys and Girls Clubs tonight, so she was on her own anyway. "I'll meet you there at seven."

It is only when Ava sees Potter standing in front of Fish that she wonders if this counts as a date. Potter is wearing jeans and a black crewneck sweater and black suede loafers without socks, even though it's November.

He is too good-looking for her, yet he beams when Ava emerges from the cab.

He nearly picks her up off the ground in his embrace. She feels the surge of desire she experienced on the Sunfish in Anguilla and then again at the Bar after her mother's wedding.

Fresh perspective, she thinks. She raises her face, and Potter doesn't hesitate. He kisses her until she feels light-headed and has to grab his arms. His sweater is so soft. It's cashmere.

Two things occur to Ava in that moment: She is going to owe Shelby dinner at the Club Car. With caviar. And no matter which job she takes, she will never have to teach the recorder again.

THE HOLIDAYS

KELLEY

It's a quiet Thanksgiving this year. Patrick, Jennifer, and the boys are going to San Francisco to spend the holiday with Jennifer's mother, Beverly, and Ava has chosen to stay in New York with Margaret, a decision that shows where her heart is. It has taken thirty years but Ava has finally—and inevitably, he supposes—turned into Margaret. On Wednesday morning, she was offered the job of her dreams, as the director of musical studies at Copper Hill School on West Seventieth Street.

Kelley writes this down word for word so he can put it in the Christmas letter.

Kevin, Isabelle, and Genevieve will be on the island and Kevin has suggested that Kelley and Mitzi allow Isabelle to cook and that they eat in the pocket-size dining room of the cottage they're renting.

Kelley is too embarrassed to express how he feels about this. He feels irrelevant; he feels like he's being replaced as patriarch. For years and years, Kelley has wished for Kevin to find his way. But now that he has—Quinns' on the Beach is an enormous success—well, he feels jealous. He's not ready to pass the baton yet and certainly not where Thanksgiving is concerned. If they eat at Kevin's house, Kevin will want to carve the turkey. The notion is outrageous!

Kelley expects Mitzi to side with him. She will say no way to eating at Kevin and Isabelle's. Mitzi *loves* Thanksgiving. She loves getting one of the sought-after fresh turkeys from Ray Owen's farm and making her famous stuffing with the challah bread, sausage, pine nuts, and dried cherries. Kelley can't imagine Mitzi allowing Isabelle to make the stuffing. What do the French know about stuffing? Nothing, that's what.

But when Kelley tells Mitzi about Kevin's invitation, she says, "What a lovely idea!"

She sounds genuine. Kelley blinks. Mitzi spent last Thanksgiving in Lenox with George. It was the nadir of her depression and she couldn't bring herself to boil a potato or end a bean and so they ended up going out to the Olde Heritage Tavern, where Mitzi cried into her cranberry relish. She definitely wants to make up for what was, essentially, a lost Thanksgiving last year, and besides, she has to keep busy. That's how she survives. She has the inn to run, but any additional distraction is welcome— Margaret's wedding in August, and Kevin and Isabelle's impending nuptials. Thanksgiving too—or so he'd thought.

"You *want* to go to Kevin's?" Kelley asks.

"Sure," Mitzi says. "It'll be fun."

"Fun?" Kelley says.

"Something new and different," Mitzi says. "They're getting married; they moved into the new house. It's only natural they would want to host us."

Natural? Kelley thinks. *Fun?* These aren't words Mitzi should be using. Their son, Bart, their *baby,* is missing. Kelley has counted on Mitzi to be the more emotionally vigilant of the two of them; she worries all the time at the maximum level so that Kelley doesn't have to. But now, instead of being thrown into a tailspin by the holiday, she's relaxed. It's almost as if she's *forgotten* about Bart or is, somehow, getting used to the agony of their circumstances. Kelley remembers when his brother, Avery, died of AIDS. His parents had been *destroyed;* his mother, Frances, especially. But the day had come, hadn't it, when Kelley had called his parents' house in Perrysburg, Ohio, and Frances had been hosting her bridge group.

Bridge group? Kelley had said. *What about Avery?*

Frances said, *Avery is with the Lord now. There's nothing I can do about that. So I might as well host bridge group.*

The next thing Mitzi says really knocks Kelley's socks off.

"If we go to Kevin's, I'll be able to do the Turkey Plunge."

"The Turkey Plunge!" Kelley says. "Since when have you been interested in doing the Turkey Plunge?"

"Since forever," Mitzi says. "It's a Nantucket tradition! But I've always been too busy cooking. This is my year. I'm doing it."

Kelley is speechless.

"Do you want to do it with me?" she asks.

"No," Kelley says. The Turkey Plunge is a fund-raiser for the Nantucket Atheneum in which scores of crazy people put on bathing suits and run into the water at Children's Beach. Nothing sounds less appealing to Kelley. That has always been true, but this year Kelley feels like a husk. He has no energy and lately has been plagued with a headache that never seems to go away. Just discussing the Turkey Plunge exhausts him so much that he wants to lie down in a dark room.

Mitzi harrumphs. She calls Isabelle to accept the invitation for Thanksgiving, then signs herself up for the Turkey Plunge.

*   *   *

Ten o'clock on the day of Thanksgiving finds Kelley bundled up in jeans, duck boots, an Irish fisherman's sweater over a turtleneck, his navy Barbour jacket over his sweater, a hat, and leather gloves standing down on the green at Children's Beach along with every other person on Nantucket, locals and visitors alike. One of the visitors is Vice President Joe Biden. Kelley has heard that Biden comes to Nantucket every Thanksgiving but he's never seen him in person until today. Kelley would love to bend the vice president's ear about Bart and the other missing Marines but the man is surrounded by a crowd ten people deep. He seems to be more popular than ever now that he's about to be replaced. If Margaret were here, Kelley would have her make the introduction, but she's not—and besides, it's Mitzi's big moment. She is out and about, chatting and schmoozing with people and reminding them all about the Christmas Eve party at the inn, which will also serve as Kevin and Isabelle's wedding reception.

"We're moving all of the furniture out of the living room," Mitzi says, "and getting a band."

The spirit of the Turkey Plunge is convivial and festive, the weather freezing cold but sunny. Kelley sees people he has known for so long they feel like family.

Mitzi pulls off her Lululemon yoga pants and her jacket and gives them to Kelley to hold. She's in an orange one-piece that Kelley has never seen before.

"That's a great suit," he says.

"Bought it just for today," she says. She kisses him on the lips and runs to line up with all the other hardy souls on the beach.

The gunshot sounds and the swimmers charge into the

water, laughing and shrieking. Mitzi is easy to pick out in her pumpkin-colored suit. Her curly hair flies out behind her as she runs, then high-steps through the water, then submerges. Kelley winces, imagining the shock and burn of water that cold. He gets Mitzi's towel ready.

When she approaches, dripping and shivering, he wraps her up and gives her a squeeze. "You are a very brave woman," he says. "Now I see where our son gets it."

Mitzi asked Kelley which of her Thanksgiving dishes he can't live without and his answer was "All of them." He loves the stuffing, the sour cream mashed potatoes, the corn pudding, the creamed onions, the butternut squash, the fiesta cranberry sauce, the snowflake rolls. But if he has to pick one, he'll pick the corn pudding, made with Bartlett's Farm corn that Mitzi bought and froze this past summer and topped with buttery Ritz crackers. To Kelley it's the ideal blend of island-grown produce and the midwestern-housewife fare that he and Avery were raised on.

And he'll also pick the fiesta cranberry sauce. Mitzi completely reinvents the dish, adding orange peel, cilantro, and jalapeño peppers. It's so addictive, Kelley craves it all year long.

"Okay," she said. "I'll make both."

When they get home from the Turkey Plunge, Mitzi goes to work in the kitchen. The TV has been left on, and the huge balloon floats of the Macy's Thanksgiving Day Parade roll past on the screen.

Margaret is there, as she is every year. And today, so is Ava. Kelley feels a sharp pain at the back of his skull. He misses Ava. He has taken her for granted all these years and now she's leaving, possibly for good. Mitzi has also accepted *this* with equanimity.

Ava's breaking up with Scott and Nathaniel is the best thing she ever did, Mitzi says now. "Ava needed to find Ava, and the Ava she found wants to move to the city. I lived in the city when I was young, and so did you. The good news is...she's teaching. I'm sure she'll come home every summer."

Summer isn't enough! Kelley thinks. He knows how unreasonable he sounds, how rigid. His head is splitting. He tells Mitzi he needs to go take a nap.

"Good idea," Mitzi says. "I'll cook and watch a little pregame, then I'll come wake you. Isabelle wants us at three."

Kelley has one of his dreams. He and Bart are in a car; Kelley is driving. They are in a desert. It looks like pictures Kelley has seen of the American Southwest but Bart keeps telling Kelley they're in Australia.

Australia? Kelley says. *That doesn't sound right. Shouldn't we be in Afghanistan?*

No, Bart says. *They got it all wrong. Everyone thought we were in Afghanistan, but we weren't.*

Kelley drives to the edge of a cliff. Far, far below are jagged, red rocks. *Is this a gorge?* Kelley asks. Bart gets out of the car. He starts to walk away.

"Kelley! *Kelley!*"

Kelley opens his eyes. His head is killing him, and that's not a euphemism. It feels like his head is trying to pull away from the rest of his body.

"Kelley!"

With effort, Kelley sits up. Mitzi? She's calling for him.

"Kelley!" she's screaming. Really screaming. Maybe her apron caught on fire or she missed a step and the corn pudding spilled out of the casserole dish all over the floor. Kelley gets out of bed and stumbles to the door. He sees Mitzi at the end of the hallway. She's wearing an apron—it's not on fire—she's crying, she's sobbing, breathless, pointing in the direction of the kitchen. What? She's holding something, Kelley sees. It's the telephone.

This is it, he thinks. This is how he's always imagined it. They have news.

Kelley falls. He hits the floor, but there is no pain. Not yet, anyway. It is dark. Quiet.

MARGARET

The Wednesday night before Thanksgiving, Margaret takes her assistant, Darcy, for a farewell dinner at Eleven Madison Park. Eleven Madison Park was recently voted the best restaurant in America, and although Margaret has long outgrown being impressed by the "best" this and the "best" that, she has to admit, this dinner is pretty unforgettable. Eleven courses with wine pairings, each course based on a food tradition of New York City. The meal starts and ends with a black-and-white cookie. The first cookie is savory; the final cookie, sweet. Margaret's favorite course is the one they eat *in the kitchen*—this, the VIP treatment because she is Margaret Quinn—which riffs on the Jewish deli. They are served tiny, open-faced Reuben sandwiches— slow-cooked corned beef with homemade sauerkraut and some kind of heavenly sauce—and a petite bottle of celery soda. When Margaret sees it, she says, "I'm sorry, *what* is this?"

Celery soda.

It's bright green and fizzy, and Margaret tastes it tentatively at first, then determines it's the most delicious, refreshing, original elixir ever to cross her taste buds. It's bursting with fresh celery flavor and it's carbonated with just a hint of sweetness. It pairs beautifully with the fatty succulence of the corned beef and the piquancy of the sauerkraut.

When she and Darcy leave, Margaret agrees that Eleven Madison Park is the best restaurant in America, but she won't be able to explain why—even to Drake—beyond gushing over the celery soda.

Margaret has to bid Darcy good-bye outside the restaurant, a moment she has been dreading. Darcy has been her assistant for four years and four months. They have been a couple longer than Margaret and Drake. Being Margaret's assistant can hardly have been easy, but Darcy is one of those super-capable, incredibly knowledgeable people who take everything in stride. She is unflappable, and if she made a mistake during her tenure, Margaret hasn't found out about it. She has never been sick, never been late, never been hungover, cranky, or cross. She has been faithful, discreet, loyal, and funny, and although she has helped Margaret with innumerable details of her personal life, she has never crossed the line into acting too "chummy." Are they friends? No, Margaret thinks. Not really. This dinner aside, they have never socialized other than at work functions. Even when Margaret was on location and Darcy traveled with her, they kept their private time private. In many ways, Darcy is closer than a friend. She is family—no, not family. She is, somehow, another manifestation of Margaret Quinn, Margaret in another, younger body.

"I'll never find another assistant like you," Margaret says. "Never."

"Margaret, stop," Darcy says. "I'll cry."

"Okay," Margaret says. She is on the verge of tears herself. "If you need me, any time, for any reason..."

"I know," Darcy says. "The same goes for me."

"Good," Margaret says, and they both laugh because they know Margaret needs Darcy far more than Darcy needs Margaret.

Darcy climbs into the taxi and waves at Margaret through the window. She is heading home to Silver Spring early tomorrow and then to Atlanta on Friday to start her new life.

Good-bye, Margaret mouths. *Good-bye.*

It's just after one o'clock the next day when Darcy calls Margaret's cell phone. Margaret is still at the parade party held every year at Lee and Ginny Kramer's apartment on Central Park West, thirteen blocks south of Margaret's apartment and twenty floors closer to the action on the street. Ava and her friend Potter are also at the party; the three of them have consumed no small amount of champagne, celebrating Ava's job at Copper Hill, which Lee and Ginny's sons, Adam and Harry, both attend. There are cheers all around, several times.

It's just when Margaret is gathering her things to leave—Drake is picking up a spectacular turkey dinner with all the trimmings from Citarella—that she sees Darcy's call come in. There is no reason for Margaret to panic, but she senses Darcy is calling to tell her something. And at one o'clock on Thanksgiving? It's something big.

"Darcy?" Margaret says. She sees Ava looking at her from across the room and she turns her back and wanders into the dining room, where there are floor-to-ceiling windows. The parade has passed but the street below is flooded with people; Raoul is around the block, waiting for Margaret and Ava. They'll have to head four blocks west to get thirteen blocks north. "Darcy, what is it?"

"My source at the Pentagon?" she says. "He called me a few seconds ago. Another soldier from the missing convoy escaped."

"Oh my gosh," Margaret says, breathless. "Was it Bart?"

"Not Bart," Darcy says. "I asked specifically. My source couldn't give me the name but he could confirm it wasn't Bart."

"Oh," Margaret says. Her spirit is in a free fall.

"But Margaret, this soldier has far more information. They're about to send out a press release. He said when he escaped that half the troops were alive and—"

"Half were dead?" Margaret says.

"Yes," Darcy says. "He gave them a whole bunch of other stuff too, I guess. Details about the surroundings, how far they'd traveled, what direction they went, what landmarks he remembers. My source says the Pentagon is going to move on the information tonight."

"Tonight," Margaret says.

"I'll call if I get anything else," Darcy says.

"Yes," Margaret says. "Thank you, Darcy."

She hangs up and tries to process what she's just heard, keeping emotion at bay. She is afraid to turn around; she doesn't want Ava to see her face until she figures out what to do. Part of her, naturally, wants to let Kelley and Mitzi enjoy their turkey. They are eating at

Kevin and Isabelle's house. But no, Margaret can't keep quiet, not this time. This is too big. Half alive, half dead. *Flip a coin,* she thinks. They're going to find the kids, all of them, either way—of this, Margaret is confident.

She swallows, takes a deep breath, and replays Darcy's exact words in her mind. Then she dials the number of the inn.

JENNIFER

Jennifer comes by her type A personality honestly: She is exactly like her mother. When Jennifer and her mother, Beverly, occupy the same space, there is always a showdown and Jennifer usually loses.

Not this year, however.

Beverly likes to dine out on holidays—Easter, Thanksgiving, Christmas. More specifically, she likes to go to the Park Tavern. Jennifer has gently but firmly shot down that idea. This year, Jennifer will cook.

"Why put yourself through so much trouble?" Beverly asks. "You've had such a tough year."

"Because it's Thanksgiving, Mother," Jennifer says. She leaves no room for argument, and Beverly backs down.

By ten o'clock, Beverly's townhouse on Nob Hill smells like home cooking. Jennifer should be humming contentedly along—the meal will be to her specifications and the quality of ingredients one can find in California is far superior to what's available at home. But Jennifer is bothered by something that happened earlier that morning. She went into her mother's bathroom to borrow dental floss and in the medicine cabinet she found a brown prescription bottle filled with Vicodin. Twenty-five pills. Jennifer held the bottle in her palm and read the label: *Beverly Barrett, for pain as needed.* What bothered Jennifer wasn't that her mother had the pills—Beverly had suffered from chronic back pain for years—but how badly Jennifer wanted to sneak a few out of the bottle for herself. She could take five or six and they would probably never be noticed missing. Right?

Jennifer had set the bottle back where she found it, but she practically hyperventilated with the effort.

And now, she can't stop thinking about the pills or about how nice it would be to get high and float through the remainder of this holiday.

Jennifer went crazy at the wine store. She bought three bottles of Round Pond sauvignon blanc, three bottles of Stags' Leap chardonnay, three bottles of Cakebread cabernet, and three bottles of Schramsberg sparkling. That gives them four bottles of wine per adult, she thinks. She also went to Cowgirl Creamery in the Ferry Building and bought an assortment of cheeses, sausages, mustard, quince paste, Marcona almonds, crackers, crisps, bread sticks, olives, pickles, and chutney. She arranges all this on a platter and brings it, along with a chilled bottle of the Schramsberg, to Patrick in the den.

She sinks down next to Patrick on the leather sofa in front of the crackling fire and the enormous TV. The games are already on.

"Whoa," Patrick says as he digs into the spread. "And you expect me to eat dinner after this?"

She doesn't need the pills. She sees Sable's kind face and

hears Sable's soothing voice saying that Jennifer does not need the pills.

She hands Patrick the champagne. "Let's open this."

"Why not?" Patrick says. "It's a holiday."

He uncorks it and pours, and they raise their glasses in a toast. "I'm thankful for you," Patrick says.

"I'm thankful for us," Jennifer says. They clink glasses and drink. Ahhh. There is nothing like the first sip of really cold champagne to make one believe everything is going to be fine.

Jennifer's phone bleeps. She sets the glass down and checks her display. She coughs. It's Norah. The text reads: *Happy turkey. I need to talk to you about something. Call me please.*

Just like that, Thanksgiving is ruined.

Jennifer fakes a smile toward her husband. "It's Sable," she says. "Wishing me a happy Thanksgiving."

"Nice of her," Patrick says, but his attention is back on the game. The Patriots are playing and nothing comes between Paddy and the Pats—except maybe a Raincoast crisp smeared with Camembert and apple chutney.

Jennifer stands up. "I should get back to the kitchen," she says. She is going right upstairs to her mother's bathroom. Three pills, she decides. Only three.

But at that moment, Patrick's phone rings.

"Hey, Kev," Patrick says. Jennifer can hear the buzz of Kevin's voice but no actual words.

"Tell him I said happy Thanksgiving," Jennifer says. She can't get out of the room fast enough.

When she is halfway up the stairs, she hears Patrick screaming, "Jennifer! Jen!"

She races back down to the den. She sees the look on Patrick's face. Thanksgiving is ruined for sure.

KEVIN

Mitzi is speaking quickly but clearly: Kelley collapsed, Mitzi has called 911, she will meet Kevin at the hospital.

"And," she says, "there has been news about Bart."

"What?" Kevin says. "What is it?"

"I'll explain at the hospital," Mitzi says.

Kevin tells Isabelle to stay put—there's a turkey in the oven and Genevieve is napping—he'll call once he figures out what is going on.

Mitzi is standing outside the emergency room, smoking a cigarette. Kevin does a double take. Mitzi doesn't smoke. But that's Mitzi and she's smoking. She says, "Left over from my days with George. You want a drag?"

"Actually, yes," Kevin says. He takes the cigarette from Mitzi and thinks how much better growing up would have been if he and Mitzi had been able to commune with each other like this every once in a while. "What are they saying?"

"He's in with the doctor."

"He just fell over?"

"Fell over," Mitzi says. "Unconscious. I couldn't wake him, though the paramedics did."

"And what's the news about Bart?"

A nurse pokes her head out the doors. "Mrs. Quinn?"

Kelley is being flown to Boston in the MedFlight helicopter. The local on-call doctor—who is probably the low man on the totem pole, working on Thanksgiving—didn't like what he saw and thought Kelley would be best served at Mass. General. Dr. Cherith will be there waiting for him.

"Dr. Cherith?" Kevin says. "His oncologist? They don't think this has anything to do with the cancer, do they?"

No one in Kevin's vicinity is able—or willing—to answer that.

Mitzi says, "I have to go too. Can you take me to the airport?"

"Yes," Kevin says. "Of course."

On the way to the airport, Mitzi tells Kevin about the phone call from Margaret. Another soldier from the missing platoon escaped. It wasn't Bart. But this young man is coherent. He has valuable intelligence about where the rest of the soldiers are being held.

"He said—" Mitzi pauses and stares out the window. "Half the soldiers are alive and half are dead."

Kevin pulls into the airport parking lot. He can see Air Force 2 out on the tarmac. The vice president is on island.

"Wait a minute. What did you say?"

"This soldier told the officers who found him that half of the other soldiers are alive and half are dead."

"Half are dead?" Kevin says. His eyes are suddenly swimming with tears. Thirty minutes ago, he was hunting for the potato masher in the utensil drawer of his rental house, and now his father is being flown in an emergency helicopter to Boston and there's a 50 percent chance his younger brother is dead.

"Half are alive," Mitzi says. Kevin pulls up to the front of the terminal to let Mitzi out. "Don't you get it, Kevin? Bart is alive."

"Is that confirmed?" Kevin asks. "Did the soldier give any names?"

"No," Mitzi says. "No names, nothing confirmed." She steps out onto the curb and smiles at Kevin. "But I'm his mother. I know."

KELLEY

Charitably, Dr. Cherith waits until Friday morning to deliver the news.

Brain cancer. Or, more correctly, prostate cancer that has metastasized to the brain. Kelley has a tumor blooming in the back of his occipital lobe, creating pressure against his skull, which was probably what caused his fall.

"Blooming?" Kelley says. "Like a flower?" He pictures a rose or a peony on the back of his head.

"The tumor has tentacles, some of them far-reaching," Dr. Cherith says. "It's not resectable."

Tentacles now, like a squid. Kelley prefers the former analogy.

"So you can't operate?" Kelley says.

"No," Dr. Cherith says.

"What can you do?"

"Well, radiation, certainly. That should shrink it. The chemo protocol for this particular kind of cancer is notoriously nasty and effective only twenty-five percent of the time."

"Kind of like our new president-elect," Kelley says.

Dr. Cherith smiles, but just barely. Honestly, Kelley is so confused and overwhelmed, he can't remember who won the election.

"I'll give you all the information about the chemo and you can make your own decision," Dr. Cherith says. "For now, I suggest radiation, much like before—thirty days."

"Just keep me alive as long as you can, Doc," Kelley says. As soon as Mitzi arrived at Mass. General, she told Kelley what she'd been screaming about right before Kelley fell over. Another soldier found, reporting that half of his fellow soldiers were alive...and half dead.

"Bart?" Kelley asked. He'd wanted to ask if Bart's specific fate had been decided, but he didn't know how.

"They're going to find him," Mitzi says. "He's coming home."

Kelley had asked for Dr. Cherith to give him the diagnosis privately so he could decide how much to tell Mitzi and the kids. Everyone is consumed with thoughts of Bart. The AP reports on the recovered soldier, Private Jonathan Mackie, on Thursday night included his quote that half of his brothers-in-arms were killed by the Bely, but half remained alive. Kelley admires Mitzi's certitude that Bart is alive, and as much as he would like to join her in this steadfast belief, he can't seem to keep his mind from visiting the dark side. What if Bart was killed? What if Bart mouthed off or otherwise angered the Bely? This is certainly possible, but Kelley thinks back on everything Bart has gone through since he enlisted. The thirteen weeks of boot camp on Parris Island, where the drill instructors broke Bart down to nothing—he referred to himself only in the third person—then built him back up into a Marine. By his own account, he excelled at his PFT (physical fitness test), running three miles in twenty minutes, doing thirty-nine pull-ups and then seventy-two crunches in sixty seconds. His basic training culminated in the Crucible, a fifty-four-hour exercise during which he was allowed to sleep for only two hours and had to hike forty-two miles with obstacles. After boot camp came the Infantry Training Battalion at Camp Lejeune, where over the course of three months he learned skilled rifle shooting. Mitzi had initially had a hard time thinking about Bart handling weapons but that had been Bart's favorite part of ITB. *Every Marine is a rifleman,* he said.

Bart had been trained by the best drill instructors, men and women far tougher than the enemy; he had learned the finest combat techniques. His body was strong, his mind stronger. He would have found a way to survive.

Kelley tells Mitzi that the cancer is back, now in his brain, and that the only treatment Dr. Cherith can recommend is thirty more days of radiation.

Her bottom lip quivers and then her chin drops. He kisses the part in her hair. She smells vaguely of cigarettes. She's back at it. But under the circumstances, Kelley really can't blame her.

"I'm going to beat it," he says.

Mitzi says something he doesn't hear. She's weeping.

"What's that?" he says. He rubs her shoulder.

"We," she says.

As with all things related to events around Bart, Kelley expects a lull to follow. It may take weeks or even months for the Pentagon to move on the intelligence they received from Private Mackie. But a scant week later, the Monday following Christmas Stroll weekend—which Kelley passed quietly while Mitzi and Isabelle tended to the guests; no parties or celebrations this year—the phone at the inn rings. It's four o'clock in the morning. Mitzi answers right away, as though she has been waiting up for the call, but she is trembling so badly, she hands the phone to Kelley.

Kelley clears his throat. "Hello?"

It's Major Dominito, calling from Washington, DC. Navy Seal Team 6 was deployed and the major reports that they have recovered all of the missing Marines, alive and dead.

The major asks Kelley if he is in a place where he can receive news about his son.

Kelley pauses before he answers. He's safe in bed with his wife. The inn is quiet; most of the Stroll guests checked out the day before. But if the major is calling to say that Bart is dead, then no—he is not in a place where he can receive that news. He will never be in a place where he can receive that news.

"Yes," he whispers. He imagines the flower blooming or the squid sinking its tentacles into his brain. He will take this diagnosis, this cancer; he will take death. *But please,* he thinks, *let Bart live.*

"Your son, Private Bartholomew James Quinn, was one of the lucky ones," the major says. "He's alive."

Kelley can't answer; he is crying too hard. This is, of course, unspeakably cruel to Mitzi, who is vibrating like a live wire next to him.

"He's alive," Kelley says, and his voice cracks. Did she hear him? Did she *understand* him? "Our son is alive."

Mitzi goes to wake Ava while Kelley calls Patrick, Kevin, and Margaret.

Bart is alive!

Thirty minutes later, Ava, Kevin, Isabelle, Genevieve, Mitzi, and Kelley are all gathered in Bart's bedroom, where the light has been on for twenty-three months, one week, and two days. They join hands and through his tears—they just won't stop—Kelley says a prayer.

Thank you, God.

MARGARET

It's the biggest news story of the year other than the election (including the election, if you ask Margaret), and it's one she reports on somberly, out of respect for the seventeen American families who each lost a soldier and a son. Inside, Margaret feels not joy but relief. *There but for the grace of God go I.*

Bart Quinn is alive. The troops have to undergo a medical evaluation at Ramstein and then a ten-day debriefing. Even so, Bart should be home by Christmas Eve—in time for Kevin's wedding.

It's a Christmas miracle, sent especially for Kelley, who is sick again, sicker, Margaret suspects, than he's letting on. If everything goes according to plan, he will see his son on Christmas.

AVA

By anyone's standards, Mitzi is a Christmas person. But this year, she goes nuts, bonkers, off the reservation, completely and insanely all out in decorating for Jesus's birth.

It's not just for Bart, she says. It's for everybody celebrating Bart's return. The entire family! Plus, Kevin and Isabelle are getting married, and the Beaulieus are coming all the way from France!

Bart is in Germany, although they've all talked to him on the phone and done video chats. His cheekbone was broken, the skin punctured; he has bruises and bandages; but still, it is Bart, Ava's baby brother, and when the family sees him for the first time, they all blubber while Bart waits with no expression on his broken face. His head is shaved; all of the surviving soldiers have lice, scabies, ringworm, and dysentery. Bart has lost sixteen pounds, which is far less than most.

They aren't allowed to ask him any questions about what happened. Not yet. So mostly the conversations are Ava, Mitzi, and Kelley filling Bart in on all the family news since he's been gone. They do not, however, say anything about Mitzi's affair with George the Santa Claus and her lost year in Lenox, nor do they tell him about Kelley's cancer, although nearly the first thing he says is "Geez, Dad, you look worse than I do."

Bart is due to arrive in Boston on December 22. Paddy, Jennifer, and the boys will pick him up and drive him to Nantucket. The Chamber of Commerce called the inn to see if they could organize a parade, give him a hero's welcome, but Kelley turned them down. He and Mitzi are united in their desire for privacy in regard to Bart's return. They just want him home—not only on Nantucket but inside the inn.

Mitzi announces that her Christmas theme this year is joy. Ava doesn't recall Mitzi having a Christmas theme in previous years but she understands how joy might be at the forefront of Mitzi's mind. Mitzi makes a Christmas playlist on her iPod that she plays on the inn-wide stereo system; it consists of twenty-five versions of "Joy to the World." At first, Ava objects on principle, but actually, the renditions are so varied that the effect is quite soothing. *And heaven and nature sing!*

Mitzi and Kelley venture out to Slosek's farm and buy a

fourteen-foot-tall Douglas fir. The tree grazes the vaulted ceiling, and Kelley has to climb a ladder to secure the top to one of the exposed beams. Ava worries about her now-frail father on the ladder and so she volunteers to decorate the tree with Mitzi, a job that takes four hours and sees them drinking nearly six poinsettias (champagne with a splash of cranberry) apiece. They try to follow Jennifer's three cardinal tree-decorating rules:

1. When you think you have enough white lights, add three more strands.
2. Glass-ball ornaments are placed all the way inside the tree, near the trunk, so that the tree appears to glow from within.
3. Showpiece and heirloom ornaments go on the ends of the branches.

In Mitzi's case, the showpiece ornaments are the hand-crafted ones she received from her mother, who made an annual ornament for family and friends for over thirty years. Mitzi then sets up her impressive nutcracker collection on the mantel amid greens and giant pinecones she ordered from Colorado. She co-opts the round mail table at the inn's entrance for her Byers' Choice carolers.

Let every heart prepare him room! All this is pretty much as it has been in previous years, before Mitzi left with George, before Bart was a Marine, before, before, before.

But...there are a bunch of new ideas!

Mitzi painstakingly wraps each and every hardback book on the shelves in contrasting plaid paper. She bakes and decorates two gingerbread houses and uses them as bookends.

She hangs huge illuminated letters over the fireplace above the nutcrackers: *J-O-Y*.

Ava smirks, thinking that the letters are for the deaf guests who haven't heard the playlist.

On her leaf-peeping trip this past fall with Kelley, Mitzi bought sap buckets, and she now plants baby evergreens in them and places them outside the front door, draped in white fairy lights, of course. Also on the porch is an artful display of a Radio Flyer sled hauling bundles wrapped in brown butcher paper and tied up with twine.

Ava and Mitzi study the porch tableau from the street. "I think it announces that this is a joyful Christmas house," Mitzi says.

There can be no doubt about that. From the outside, the inn is a stunner. There is an enormous wreath on the front door illuminated by a spotlight and in every window, a smaller wreath dangling from burgundy velvet ribbons over a single lit candle.

"You've done a good job, Mitzi," Ava says, squeezing her stepmother's arm.

"I'm nowhere close to finished," Mitzi says.

Mitzi hangs a pair of antique skis in the hallway. She has replaced the hall rugs with candy-cane-striped runners, and one day when Ava comes home from school, she finds even her bedroom has been decorated. There is a wreath hanging from her scrolled walnut headboard, and her bed has been dressed up with a red flannel comforter and crisp white sheets with red piping. On her dresser is an arrangement of greens, pinecones, and holly, and next to that a fat white pillar candle that Ava recognizes as Mitzi's favorite scent, Fraser fir. Are all of the bedrooms like this? Ava has to check.

Yes! Kevin and Isabelle's former bedroom has been

decked out with the Christmas linens and headboard wreath, as has Kelley and Mitzi's and...Bart's! (Ava can't believe Mitzi was brave enough to decorate Bart's room. Despite the fact that it *still* smells vaguely of pot smoke, it has been treated like a shrine.) But an even bigger surprise is that the room that used to be Genevieve's nursery has been transformed into a Christmas workshop. Mitzi bought a pine table and is using it as a wrapping station, but along with the predictable paper, bows, and tags are stuffed elves sitting on chairs and chilling on the windowsills. There's a new red brocade wingback chair and a matching footstool where another elf sits, staged so it looks like he's stringing a popcorn garland. And in the corner of the room is yet another Christmas tree, this one decorated with tiny musical instruments—a snare drum, a violin, a harp, a harmonica.

But no recorder, Ava notices.

When Ava calls Potter that evening, she says, "I feel like I'm living at the North Pole." She explains the wrapped books and gingerbread houses, the antique skis and Santa's workshop. She has also noticed that the Christmas china is out, that there is mistletoe hanging in the kitchen, and that on the windowsill over the sink someone has arranged Scrabble tiles to read MERRY CHRISTMAS. By the back door is a forest-green stepladder on which Mitzi has secured all of the Christmas cards and pictures she has received so far.

"I can't wait to see it," Potter says. "I could use a little holiday cheer."

"Next week!" Ava says. She knows Potter's December has been anything but joyful. He's dealing with final exams, and his son, PJ, is spending the holiday with his mother and the British teaching assistant. They are traveling to Stratford-upon-Avon to celebrate a Shakespear-ean Christmas.

"In front of the Yule log?" Ava asks. "Why did Shake-speare never write a Christmas play?"

"He did. *Twelfth Night*," Potter says glumly.

Ava loves Potter's erudition!

"I'm sorry I'm in such a funk," Potter says. "I'll feel bet-ter the second I can hold you."

When he says things like this, Ava melts. The first night she spent with Potter—back in New York over Thanksgiving—she confessed that she thought he was too good-looking for her. Oh, how he had laughed! He'd wiped tears from the cor-ners of his eyes and said, "There isn't a man alive who is too good-looking for you, Ava. Not Clooney. Not Tatum Channing."

Ava had grinned. "Channing Tatum."

"Him either." Potter had taken Ava's face in his hands and said, "I think you are the most beautiful, most captivating creature I have ever laid eyes on and I've thought that since I passed you running in Anguilla."

"Stop," she said.

He had kissed her deeply, then carried her off to bed.

She is taking things slowly with Potter. This is her new, adult self in action; she doesn't fall all the way in love imme-diately, as she's done in the past. She preserves her privacy, her personhood. But there's no denying she's besotted, and his feelings seem to match or exceed her own.

A week before Christmas, Ava admits to Shelby that she's officially seeing Potter. He's going to be her date for Kevin and Isabelle's wedding and not just because he has a talent for making Quinn family nuptials fun. He's stay-ing through Christmas. At first, Potter felt bad about leav-ing Gibby alone but then Ava suggested Potter bring him up to Nantucket as well. *The more the merrier,* Ava said. *And when you get here, you'll see I mean that.* Potter agreed this was the ideal solution and he booked Gibby a room at the Castle, which is where George and Mary Rose are staying. And surprise, surprise! George is bringing over his 1931 Model A fire engine for the first time in three years, and this will be the vehicle that transports Kevin and Isabelle from the Siasconset Union Chapel to the inn, with George dressed as Santa Claus behind the wheel.

"It's a little scary," Shelby says. "Your family's devotion to Christmas."

"Tell me about it," Ava says. "Anyway, I owe you dinner at the Club Car."

"With caviar," Shelby says.

They get dressed up and go the following night. Ava wears a green velvet Betsey Johnson dress that she's owned for years but only recently has been able to fit into—talk about Christmas joy!—and Shelby wears red. The Club Car is all decked out for Christmas and it smells of garlic and rosemary. The piano is stationed in the back, as ever, the pianist piecing together a medley of carols.

"*Anything* but 'Joy to the World,'" Ava says. "I'll even take 'Jingle Bells.'"

"Wow, that is *not* like you," Shelby says.

The maître d' seats them in the front window. "You two are the prettiest window dressing I could ask for," he says.

"But more important, we're smart," Shelby says.

Ava smiles down at the table. Being a mother has not softened Shelby in the slightest.

They order champagne, naturally, and then two ounces of osetra caviar, which comes with all of the usual accoutrements—buckwheat blini, chopped onion, capers, egg whites, egg yolks, and crème fraîche—as well as a bottle of vodka, nestled in a block of ice, from which the waiter pours them each a shot. And then, maybe because they are pretty or maybe because they are smart, he pours them each another shot, on the house.

Ho-ho-ho! Ava's head is instantly spinning, so much so that she thinks she sees Scott and Roxanne by the maître d's stand. She blinks and chases the vodka taste out of her mouth with a sip of crisp, cold champagne.

It *is* Scott and Roxanne. Roxanne is wearing a black dress. Ava heard that she has worn black every day since losing the baby. And she's wearing black stiletto heels. Some people, it seems, never learn.

Scott waves. Ava waves. Shelby glances over her shoulder and groans.

"It's not a problem," Ava says. "He doesn't faze me anymore. And neither does she."

"Really?" Shelby says. She builds herself a loaded caviar bite, and her eyelids flutter closed in ecstasy as she eats it. "I'm sorry, what were we talking about?"

"I'm over Scott," Ava says. It's true; she sees him and feels nothing. This past Friday afternoon he dressed up as Santa Claus for the final assembly before break and he handed out candy canes and chocolate coins, and Ava gazed upon him and felt...nothing. A couple days before that, he had come to school wearing his ugly Christmas sweater, the one with the light-up tulle Christmas tree on the front that he had bought solely to please Ava. The one he had worn to her Ugly Christmas Sweater Caroling party. The one he had worn when he accompanied Roxanne to Nantucket Cottage Hospital and then Mass General after she gruesomely broke her ankle while crossing Federal Street.

That sweater had so many memories attached to it—both good and bad—and yet when Ava saw Scott wearing it, she had felt...nothing.

"I hope he and Roxanne are happy together," Ava says. "I hope they try to have a baby again."

"Not likely," Shelby says. "I heard she's moving to California soon, before the end of the school year."

"Is she?" Ava says. Not even this juicy tidbit piques her interest. If Roxanne moves to California, Scott will be single once again. All Ava feels is a twinge of sympathy for Scott— but honestly, not much. He's a good guy. He'll find someone else soon enough.

Scott and Roxanne are seated at a table somewhere behind them, but Ava doesn't even bother to sneak a peek. She doesn't scrutinize the expression on Scott's face or analyze his demeanor or wonder what he orders to drink. Maybe Roxanne *is* moving to California and this is a farewell dinner, or maybe they're just out celebrating the holiday. Ava doesn't care!

She studies the menu. "I'm going to get the beef Wellington," she says. "And then, let's go sing."

JENNIFER

The texts from Norah Vale pop up on Jennifer's phone at the worst possible moments. The first was on Thanksgiving, but it was instantly eclipsed by the phone call from Kevin with the double-whammy news of Kelley's collapse and another soldier from Bart's platoon found.

A week later, they know that Kelley's cancer has metasta-sized to his brain and that Bart is alive. A mixed bag of news if ever there was one. Patrick has chosen to focus only on the positive: Bart is alive and coming home in time for Kevin and Isabelle's wedding and Christmas. And Kelley will bat-tle his cancer just the way he's battled all the other hardships of the past few years.

"My father is a warrior," Patrick says.

Jennifer hears the respect in Patrick's voice, which serves to mask his fear. Kelley is only in his early sixties, but he's mortal just like everyone else.

For the kids' sake, Jennifer adopts Patrick's mind-set. They don't tell the boys about Kelley's cancer. All they announce is that Uncle Bart has been found and is on his way home. "Uncle Bart is a hero, a real-life hero who experienced unknown horrors while defending our coun-try," they say. Patrick and Jennifer hammer this home; their kids need something to honor other than their video games.

Norah's second text comes while Jennifer is decorating a client's house for Christmas. She had such success putting her own home on the Beacon Hill Holiday House Tour that decorating for Christmas has become a cottage industry within Jennifer's already-booming interior design business. She has twelve clients across Boston and the suburbs who want her to deck their halls. Jennifer isn't in a position to turn away any business. She is grateful for all the clients who stuck with her through Patrick's incarceration, and she still lives in fear that rumors of her pharmaceutical addiction might get out.

At the moment, she is decorating a townhome for a cou-ple in the South End who are throwing a huge party in a few hours. This project has turned out to be more fun than

Jennifer anticipated. The couple favor a mid-twentieth-century style, and too much is not enough for Peter and Ken, so out come the white Christmas trees decorated with psychedelic glass balls and on the wall hangs a display of holiday-themed Jell-O molds.

Brenda Lee plays on the blue Bakelite turntable—"Rockin' Around the Christmas Tree"—while Ken shakes up some martinis and Peter prepares the ham, decorating it with pineapple rings and maraschino cherries.

"I wish you could stay," Peter says.

"Me too," Jennifer says. She loves this couple, loves the vibe of their home and all of the authentic details. The presents under the tree are sleek and color-coordinated. There's a pile of royal-blue presents, a pile of hot-pink presents, a pile of amethyst-purple presents.

Christmas comes in all shapes and sizes, Jennifer thinks. *All colors, all eras.* She would love to don a shimmery minidress, put on chunky heels and shimmery earrings, and drink martinis and eat deviled eggs and chicken livers wrapped in bacon.

Eartha Kitt sings "Santa Baby."

But tonight, Jennifer and Patrick are going out alone. They both miss the lavish holiday party that Everlast Investments throws at the Four Seasons, so they have decided to throw a "company party" of their own. They're going for drinks at Sonsie and then having dinner at No. 9 Park.

As Jennifer is putting the finishing touches on Peter and Ken's vintage-Christmas-card collage, her phone pings.

She checks it eagerly, half hoping it's Paddy telling her he's running behind with work so that she can stay for a few more minutes and enjoy a martini or two. But no. It's Norah.

The text says: *Are you by any chance coming to Nantucket for Stroll? I really need to talk to you.*

Stroll, Jennifer thinks. That's right. Tonight is the Friday of Stroll weekend on Nantucket.

Burl Ives sings "Have a Holly Jolly Christmas."

"I just love the way records sound on this turntable," Peter says.

Jennifer gives him a blank look, then she stares at the message on her phone. Stroll weekend last year was when all of Jennifer's troubles began. She wanted oxy and Ativan, and who, of all people, supplied her habit? Argh! Jennifer wants to go back in time to Stroll weekend of last year and do everything differently.

"Are you okay?" Ken asks. He hands her a martini.

Jennifer slips her phone into her pocket and fakes a smile. "Yes!" she says.

"She wants to leave so she can go on a date with her hubby," Peter says. "Let her go already."

What does Norah want to talk to her about? Should Jennifer respond or just ignore this text as she did the last one?

"You can go," Ken says. "But this martini is a work of art. Take it home and enjoy it as you get dressed. I'll get you a cup."

"And take a deviled egg!" Peter calls out from the kitchen.

Andy Williams sings "It's the Most Wonderful Time of the Year."

The third text from Norah comes as Jennifer is wrapping the boys' gifts on her bed and bingeing on *Bloodline*. *Bloodline* comes at the recommendation of Sable; former addicts know all the best shows, Sable insisted, and Jennifer laughed, thinking this was probably true. It's eleven o'clock at night a week before Christmas, and Paddy is still in the home office, working. Jennifer brought him a glass of scotch and a piece of gingerbread with lemon sauce an hour earlier while he pored over the day's market activity. He has raised thirty-two million for his hedge fund so far. This is going to happen, he assures Jennifer. This is going to be a success.

When Jennifer's phone pings so late, she assumes it's her mother in California, who is infamous for disregarding the time difference.

When Jennifer sees that it's Norah, she gasps, as she might have at a stranger's face appearing in her dark bedroom window.

The text says, simply, *Jennifer.*

"What?" Jennifer whispers. "What do you want?"

A second text follows: *I'll be in Boston the next few days. Call me, please.*

Jennifer nearly screams. Norah is coming to Boston. Norah is going to...what? Stalk Jennifer? Knock on the front door or sit in her menacing black truck, engine idling, out on Beacon Street? Will she trail Jennifer as she takes the kids to school? Will she harass Jennifer in front of the other parents? Will Jennifer's dirty little secret get out? Will Norah harm Jennifer or threaten the children?

This has to stop, Jennifer thinks. She holds her phone gingerly, like it's a ticking time bomb. She types in: *Leave me alone. Please.* But that makes her sound like she's a victim, pleading, groveling. She doesn't send it.

Jennifer deletes the texts, just as she deleted the other two texts; she can just pretend they never existed. She can block Norah's number on her phone. She should have done this back in August!

What does Norah *want?* She knows Jennifer got caught

by Kevin and Paddy and she surely must guess that Jennifer has been through counseling. Norah should count herself lucky that Jennifer didn't go to the police!

She should go to the police now, Jennifer thinks. To Paddy first, then the police. She should have kept the texts to turn over as evidence!

But another, calmer part of Jennifer's psyche encourages her not to overreact. Norah is, no doubt, just after some money. Jennifer should continue to ignore her. Eventually, she'll go away.

Jennifer wraps the last present—a black leather belt with a silver buckle, for Bart. Mitzi has said he's lost weight and none of his clothes will fit. *An American hero needs to keep his pants up,* Jennifer thinks. Then she laughs. Thoughts of Norah fade away.

KELLEY

His radiation oncologist has granted him a week's reprieve over Christmas. He doesn't have to report for his final treatments until December 27.

He may skip those anyway. The radiation isn't working. He has inhabited this body for more than sixty years and *he* holds the ultimate authority over it—not his doctors. He knows the cancer is growing, sinking its tentacles deeper and deeper into his brain. He's dizzy all the time and needs to hold on to the rail as he descends the stairs. He can barely hear out of his left ear, a development he's trying to conceal by cocking his head when someone is speaking to him. And the headaches are…stupendous. They are impossible to endure without medication, but the pain medication makes him loopy and, of course, he doesn't want to become addicted, like Jennifer.

Although, he reasons, what does it matter if he becomes addicted now? The end is coming. He can feel it.

He doesn't share this knowledge with anyone. Nobody wants to hear it! Everyone expects Kelley to battle, to wield his mighty sword and fight off the failure of his body. Plus, everyone is distracted. It's Christmastime! Kevin and Isabelle are getting married! Bart is coming home! Ava is moving to the city to embark on her new career! Patrick is starting his act two, a hedge fund where he will be his own boss!

Kelley is so fortunate to have stood at the head of such an incredible family. When he passes, he can do so knowing everyone is safe.

But enough maudlin thoughts.

The house is decorated from the floorboards to the rafters. Kelley can't enter or leave a room without hearing a merry jingle (Mitzi has hung sleigh bells from every doorknob throughout the inn). He smells the pot of beef bourguignon on the stove, ideal for this chilly night. (Because Mitzi was a non-red-meat-eater for so long, every time they eat beef, it feels like a Christmas miracle.) Bart is supposed to fly from Germany to Washington on the twenty-second and from there to Boston on the twenty-third. He will be on Nantucket Friday night, which is cutting it a little close for Mitzi's taste, but what can they do? The mere thought of seeing his son, hugging him, holding him makes Kelley almost weep. Bart has a wound on his face in the exact spot that Kelley dreamed he had a tattoo of a star. This is uncanny, so eerie that

Kelley is certain that no one will understand or appreciate his prescience, so he keeps it to himself. He wonders if the cancer in his brain is, somehow, giving him a sixth sense.

The closer Bart gets to home, the more impatient to see him Kelley grows. He has waited twenty-three months, but these last three days are torture.

He won't waste a second of his holiday worrying about his health, he decides. He will simply enjoy this Christmas as though it were his last.

MARGARET

When was it that Margaret said that her favorite news stories were about the weather?

On the twentieth of December, she gets the first warning from the meteorological team at CBS, and this warning is given in person by Dougie Clarence, the new, young hipster face of weather at the network. Dougie comes over and sits on Margaret's desk. He's wearing a fedora, a plaid vest, pants that reach only to his ankles, and lace-up loafers with no socks. His shirtsleeves are rolled up and he sports a goatee. Every woman in New York City under the age of thirty-five loves Dougie. Margaret loves Dougie. If Ava weren't involved with Potter, the first man Margaret would have set her up with was Dougie Clarence.

However much Margaret enjoys Dougie's company, though, finding him sitting on her desk five days before Christmas and three days before she's supposed to fly to

Nantucket for her son's wedding is not good. Dougie visits Margaret only when he has an urgent weather bulletin worthy of the national news.

"To what do we owe this honor, Mr. Clarence?" she asks.

"I've been missing you," Dougie says. He gives Margaret a hug and a kiss on the cheek.

"And I you," Margaret says. Dougie hasn't been to see her even once this year. The weather has been virtually perfect.

"But that's not why I'm here," Dougie says.

Margaret's spirits fall. Maybe it's the weather in the Midwest. Maybe he wants her to report on the drought in California—again. Maybe Mount St. Helens is about to blow. That would be exciting! Margaret has never reported on a good volcano story.

"I'm here because we are about to get pounded," Dougie says.

"We?" Margaret says. "Pounded?"

"The Northeast Corridor," Dougie says. "Blizzard."

"When?" Margaret asks.

"Tomorrow night, Thursday, Friday," Dougie says. "The good news is it should be mostly over by Christmas Eve. The bad news is it's I-95 from Washington to Boston."

"And the airports," Margaret says.

"I don't like to use the term *hundred-year storm*," Dougie says. "But in this case . . ."

"Does it have a name?" Margaret asks.

"Elvira," Dougie says.

Elvira.

Margaret looks at the briefs her new assistant, Jennifer, left her: ISIS cells suspected in the Netherlands and Denmark; the changing social landscape of Washington with the new administration (internally, Margaret groans; if there's anything she dislikes more than election news, it's postelection news); and…the eighteen surviving Marines making their way home.

Marines on their way home. Bart.

"Are we talking a C block?" Margaret asks. "B block?"

Dougie shrugs. "If you're asking me…an A block."

"That bad?" Margaret says.

"That bad."

Margaret understands only the rudimentary basics of the science behind snowstorms. It all starts with the sun. The sun heats the earth unequally…direct sunshine in tropical regions, and low-angle sun at the poles. Heat builds up in the tropics and creates an imbalance in temperature from tropics to poles. The atmosphere doesn't like this and tries to transport heat toward the poles.

So why do the biggest snowstorms form off the coast of North Carolina, track up to Long Island, and pound the Northeast? Because there is a perfect cocktail of weather ingredients there that's found nowhere else in America. Cold, dense Canadian air pours southward while warm, moist air carried by the Gulf Stream ocean current tracks northward. Every now and again, the jet stream, a ribbon of strong airflow, takes a dip to the south, and through very complicated thermodynamics (that extend well beyond what was covered in the "rocks for jocks" class Margaret took at the University of Michigan) creates a low-pressure system. This low-pressure system intensifies over the warm Gulf waters, and the warm, moist air rises and flows over the cold Canadian air. The winds flow counterclockwise around the low-pressure center, and this causes the northeasterly winds to push the snow back into New England. This is how we get the term *nor'easter*—it is the wind's direction during the most intense part of a storm. In winter, this storm becomes a blizzard.

"It's expected to bomb out," Dougie says.

"Translation?" Margaret says.

"The storm will strengthen with extreme rapidity," Dougie says. "The low-pressure center will drop like a bomb."

They are predicting a foot of snow in Washington and up to thirty inches in Boston, sustained winds of forty-five to fifty miles per hour, and—Dougie suspects—that rarest of weather phenomena: thundersnow. Minutes after Dougie leaves Margaret's office, the National Weather Service issues a winter storm warning for the entire Northeast. Amtrak suspends service on December 22 and 23. Delta, Jet Blue, United, and American cancel six hundred flights, leaving over ten thousand passengers scrambling for alternative transportation.

Margaret is sitting at her desk at the studio on Wednesday when the snow starts to fall. She has released Raoul from his driving duties until after the holidays. Drake calls and says he's rented a Ford Expedition and volunteers to drive himself and Margaret up to Hyannis. For as long as Margaret has known Drake, she has never seen him drive. He takes taxis.

"Are you sure?" Margaret asks.

"I'm sure," Drake says. "But you have to tell Lee you're not broadcasting tomorrow. We need to leave tonight, Margaret, as soon as you're done."

"Oh," Margaret says. She already asked to take off the Friday night before her usual weeklong hiatus over Christmas. Can she ask for yet *another* night off? Margaret is sixty-one years old. She has been the anchor of the *CBS Evening News* for fourteen years. She's not worried about job security as much as she's plagued by a sense of duty. Millions of Americans will, likely, have their Christmas ruined by this storm, and

Margaret feels compelled to be the one in the chair reporting on it.

But Kevin is her son and he's getting married.

She feels torn in two, just as she used to when the kids were young. "What about your surgeries?" Margaret asks Drake. "Surely you can't leave a day early."

"Jim and Terry are covering them for me," Drake says. "They're both staying in the city."

No more excuses, Margaret thinks.

She calls Lee. "I need tomorrow night off too, Lee," she says.

"Margaret," he says.

"You can't make me feel any guiltier than I already feel," Margaret says.

He's silent. She hates when Lee is silent.

"Kevin is getting married," she says.

"On Saturday," Lee says. "I gave you Friday off to accommodate you going to Kevin's wedding. That was my gift. I can't let you go Thursday. The viewers want Margaret Quinn. The advertisers want Margaret Quinn. People turn on the TV and see Julian and they change the channel."

"Find someone who's more appealing than Julian!" Margaret says.

"That's a conversation for another day," Lee says. "This conversation is about you taking off Thursday night and the answer is no."

Margaret fills with fury, an emotion so foreign to her that she doesn't quite know how to process it. She is Margaret Quinn, one of the most esteemed television journalists in the nation, if not the world. And yet she still has to answer to a man, Lee Kramer, head of the network, a person she considers a friend.

Margaret takes a breath. Lee is her friend, but this is

business. The advertisers pay Margaret's salary. She has to stay and do her job.

"Okay," she says, and then she hangs up so she can call and give Drake the bad news.

KELLEY

What we need is a sleigh," Mitzi says. "And eight reindeer."

She is standing just outside the back door of the kitchen smoking a cigarette, and Kelley is allowing it. The snow is falling slowly but relentlessly—big, fat, wet, heavy flakes, the kind you get when the temperature is hovering around the thirty-degree mark. An apron of snow is collecting on the floor and all the heat is escaping from the kitchen, which is strewn with hotel pans and dishes set up by the caterers in anticipation of the wedding reception. It's too chaotic to cook in. Kelley had wanted to get takeout Thai food but it's snowing so hard he can't even make it to Siam to Go.

Kelley and Mitzi are on Nantucket, and Kevin and Isabelle are on Nantucket, and the priest, Father Paul, is on Nantucket. He arrived on the noon boat that day and is staying at the church rectory.

The Beaulieus' plane has taken off; they're scheduled to land in Boston at midnight. Paddy volunteered to go get them, and in the morning, Jennifer and the boys and the Beaulieus will drive to Hyannis and put their car on the 2:45 slow boat. Paddy will stay in Boston and wait for Bart.

Bart's flight from Germany was rerouted to Reykjavik, Iceland, because Dulles was shut down due to the storm.

Kelley was able to talk to Bart, but only briefly. Bart wasn't sure what the flight status was; he and the other guys were planning to hit the airport bar.

"All the chicks here are blond," Bart said.

Kelley was cheered by the fact that Bart finally sounded like himself, but he had wanted to remind Bart that no matter how cold the beer or how beautiful the blondes, Bart needed to focus on getting home.

Margaret is in New York. Drake is going to drive her up Thursday after her broadcast, so they should be on Nantucket first thing Friday morning.

Assuming the boats go. And the planes.

Mitzi holds out the last of her cigarette. "You want?"

He does want, very much, but he has a vision of one puff hurrying his cancer along to the point where his head shatters like a glass ornament hitting the stone floor.

"No, thank you," he says. He walks out onto the deck to look up into the sky at the thousands of descending snowflakes, no two exactly alike. If you can believe that, then why not also believe that Santa Claus and his reindeer might pick Bart up in Reykjavik and deliver him home?

He leads Mitzi inside and closes the door behind them. "Sit down," Kelley says. "I'll make grilled cheese."

JENNIFER

She has a reservation for her family and their BMW X5 on the steamship leaving Hyannis at 2:45 on Thursday but then that boat gets canceled, as does the 8:15 p.m. boat, and the

Beaulieus haven't arrived anyway. Their flight from Orly was rerouted to Nova Scotia.

Bart, meanwhile, is in Reykjavik, Iceland.

"I've always wanted to go to Reykjavik," Paddy says. "Maybe we'll just blow off Kevy's wedding and I'll meet Bart there."

"Not funny," Jennifer says. She is presently without her sense of humor. Paddy is in the home office wearing a Santa hat. He seems perfectly relaxed. He doesn't have to worry about three rambunctious boys killing zombies in the family room or the missing parents of their soon-to-be sister-in-law or a car whose backseat and Thule carrier is crammed full of presents, compromising the crisp beauty of Jennifer's wrapping and the perfection of her bows. Jennifer had everything packed and ready to go and now she's being delayed, maybe for as long as twenty-four hours. She is going to have to run to Whole Foods to get groceries for dinner, but Beacon Hill is experiencing a whiteout. She's not sure she can make it the three blocks to Cambridge Street on foot.

She turns on the TV but that just makes things worse. NECN is showing footage of the long snake of cars on Route 3, tractor-trailers jackknifed, all of the carnage barely visible through the snow.

Jennifer rummages through the fridge and cabinets; she has eggs, a pound of bacon, half a gallon of milk. They could always have breakfast for dinner.

Then the power goes out.

There is a shout from Patrick—his computer!

There is a blended shout from the boys—the TV! Their game!

Jennifer goes to the big picture window in the living room. She stands next to their now-dark Christmas tree, looking across Boston Common. The common is dark; every house up and down Beacon Street is dark. The cars on Park Street and Tremont honk in unified panic. Have the traffic lights gone out? Does that ever happen? All Jennifer can see is snow and more snow.

Her phone pings. She jumps, then checks the display. It's Norah.

No, Jennifer thinks.

The text says: *Are you coming to Nantucket for Christmas?*

Paddy's voice out of the darkness makes Jennifer jump again. Instinctively, she tucks her phone in her pocket.

"Do we have candles?" he asks.

KEVIN

They should have eloped. They could have left Genevieve with Kelley and Mitzi, flown to St. Barts for four or five days, and come home a married couple.

Genevieve is teething; whenever Kevin or Isabelle puts her down, she starts to cry.

Isabelle has spent at least fifteen minutes every hour for the past ten hours on the phone with one or the other of her parents. They are stuck in Nova Scotia. Nova Scotia! The good news is that they have befriended a couple from Montreal who speak French; the bad news is that Logan is closed for the foreseeable future, and even if Logan were open, Nantucket is unreachable—no boats, no planes, coming or going.

They should have eloped.

Kelley and Mitzi are, predictably, worried about Bart. Bart is in Iceland, getting drunk and wooing women with his uniform and his war wounds. Kevin doesn't have the luxury of worrying about Bart right now. He has two females crying in his house; both of them want their parents.

Kevin picks up Genevieve and rubs her back. He takes the teething ring out of the freezer; this works for thirty seconds as Genevieve mad-gnaws on the thing like a dog with a bone, which is just long enough for Kevin to pour three fingers of Jameson into a highball glass, dip a clean washcloth into the whiskey, then rub the cloth on Genevieve's gums. Jameson was what worked when Paddy and Kevin were teething, Kelley has confided. This explains some things.

"Kevin, *mon dieu!*" Isabelle says. She snatches the whiskey washcloth out of his hands.

Caught, Kevin thinks.

Genevieve starts to cry.

Before Isabelle can admonish him, her phone rings. It's her father. They will be in Nova Scotia overnight, he says. Sleeping in the terminal. Logan will not open until tomorrow morning at the earliest.

Isabelle takes the phone into the bedroom and shuts the door.

Kevin is tempted to give the whiskey another try, but instead, he brings Genevieve into the living room and turns on the TV. His mother is broadcasting and immediately Genevieve quiets down. She points at the screen.

"That's right," Kevin says. "It's Mimi."

Margaret has been joined this evening by some kid who looks like he's stepped off the pages of *GQ*. It's the meteorologist Dougie, and he is delivering the bad news. The blizzard will reach its maximum force tonight or tomorrow morning. Hardest hit will be New York City, Long Island, coastal Connecticut, Rhode Island, Boston, Cape Cod, Martha's Vineyard, and Nantucket.

Ha! Kevin thinks. He feels a childish joy any time Nantucket is mentioned on TV. It's absurd.

"These areas can expect eighteen to twenty-four inches of snow," Dougie says. The kid looks positively aglow. Margaret, although lovely in an ivory wrap dress, looks exactly like a woman who is about to sit for ten hours—*minimum*—in atrocious traffic inching northward in a car piloted by an inexperienced driver.

During the final seconds of the broadcast, when newspeople usually smile inanely at the camera, the meteorologist Dougie bursts into song: "White Christmas." He does sound a little like Bing Crosby. Kevin snaps off the set, and Genevieve starts to cry.

They should have eloped.

GEORGE

He's no stranger to New England winters and he's been coming to Nantucket at Christmastime for nearly fifteen years, so he's learned a few things. He and Mary Rose stay ahead of the storm. They drive George's 1931 Model A fire engine onto the steamship at 2:45 on Wednesday, and the man who helps them park it on the boat says to George, "You're smart. This is the last boat that'll go for days."

"You think?" George says.

"I know," the man says, looking up at the sky, which does indeed look white and heavy, like a feather pillow about to burst.

George and Mary Rose check into their room at the Castle. The hotel is cheerfully decorated for the holidays. Johnny Mathis sings "Sleigh Ride." The front-desk clerk, Livingston—George remembers him from last year—says he has a suite available and Livingston can offer it to George at the same rate as the room he booked because George is a return guest. "Wonderful!" George says, and he lets out a robust "Ho-ho-ho!" turning every head in the lobby.

"Shall we call Kelley and Mitzi and tell them we got here early?" Mary Rose asks. "Maybe they can meet us at Lola for sushi tonight."

"I want you all to myself tonight," George says. "Room service and Christmas movies."

"It's a Wonderful Life!" Mary Rose says.

That it is, George thinks. His hats were featured in the shopping guide of the holiday issue of *Vogue* and the spike in business was exactly what George needed in order to buy Mary Rose a two-carat diamond engagement ring.

He has the room-service waiter place the velvet box under a silver dome so when Mary Rose lifts it off, expecting calamari, she sees the box instead.

She shrieks. She trembles. She opens the box and sees the ring, and tears stand on her long lovely lashes.

Because of his new exercise regime, George is able to bend down on one knee. "Will you marry me?" George asks. "Will you be my Mrs. Claus?" He can't believe the difference a year makes, never mind two years. Two years ago, Kelley had caught George and Mitzi kissing in room 10, and

George's world had gone into a tailspin. Then, last year, he had broken up with Mitzi and met Mary Rose. He's a little old to believe in meant-to-be but he's old enough to know that he wants to live out his days with this delightful, curvaceous redheaded creature right here. She makes him so, so happy.

Mary Rose throws her arms around George. "Yes!" she says.

AVA

She told Potter she would pick him and Gibby up at the ferry on Wednesday evening, but Potter calls to say a guy he met on the boat has offered him and Gibby a ride to the inn so Ava should just sit tight. It has started to snow; the boat they just disembarked from wouldn't be going back to Hyannis, Potter reports.

Uh-oh, Ava thinks. Paddy and Jennifer, the boys, Isabelle's parents, Margaret and Drake, and Bart. All of them are on the wrong side of this news.

Ava can't worry about everyone else; they'll get here when they get here. She is excited to see Potter. She is still in the stage of major butterflies and although she knows she should go into her bedroom and read or play carols on the piano until Potter arrives, she stands out on the front porch, waiting. The front of the house looks *so* pretty with the tree twinkling through the window and the sled with its bundles and all of the wreaths and candles.

Joy, Ava thinks. As she waits for her new beau to arrive, she feels pure, unadulterated joy.

A familiar truck pulls up in front of the inn and Ava blinks.

What?

It's Nathaniel's truck. She recognizes the sticker from the Bar in the back window and the dent above the wheel. What is *Nathaniel* doing here? Ava's mind is racing. She receives a text or two from him each week; Ava has told him that she's moving to New York City in June to start a new job, but she hasn't told him what or where the job is, and she hasn't told him about Potter. She needs to get him out of here before Potter arrives, which is sure to be any second.

Nathaniel turns off the ignition. *No!* Ava thinks. *Not okay!* Nathaniel is going to want to catch up. He must be on Nantucket for Christmas? Ava had been sure he would go back to New Canaan for Christmas to see his parents, his sister and her kids, and his pathetic old girl-friend Kirsten Cabot. He has said nothing about return-ing to the island, and although he still has a cottage here, it seems unfair that he would show up without warning.

Then a horrifying thought enters Ava's mind: Nathaniel and Kevin are friends; is Nathaniel on Nantucket so he can come to the wedding and attend the reception at the inn on Christmas Eve?

Eeeeeeeeeeeee!

"Hey!" Nathaniel calls out with a wave. He goes to the back door of his truck and opens it. He extends a hand, and an elderly gentleman steps out.

Ava's eyes narrow. She has seen this gentleman before. It's…*Gibby*. She realizes this just as she sees Potter get out of the passenger side.

Oh no.

Potter grins and waves like…well, like a little kid at Christmas. Ava wants to return the enthusiasm but she's too addled by Nathaniel. *Nathaniel* was the guy who offered Potter and Gibby a ride to the inn. Naturally. Because Ava is the object of some curse where her love life will forever be an obstacle course.

She hurries down the steps to help Gibby.

"Hello, Gibby!" she says loudly, not because Gibby is hard of hearing but because she wants Nathaniel to realize these are not random guests of the inn. "Welcome to Nantucket!"

"Hello, my dear. Thank you for having me."

"Our pleasure!" she says. She holds Gibby's arm as he ascends the stairs. She visualizes Potter following behind with their luggage and Nathaniel disappearing with a wave and a "Merry Christmas!"

But when Ava and Gibby reach the safety of the porch and Ava turns around, she sees that both Potter and Nathaniel are heading up the stairs.

Whom to greet first?

There is only one answer to that question. Ava throws her arms around Potter's neck and kisses him so that there can be no misunderstanding the nature of their relationship. When Potter releases Ava, she turns to Nathaniel. He seems unfazed.

"Hey, stranger," he says and he hugs Ava. Tightly.

"Hey, stranger, yourself," she says. "I didn't know you were coming."

"It's a surprise," Nathaniel says.

Yes, it certainly is.

"I thought I might have Scott to contend with," Nathaniel says. "But I see my competition this year is taller. And better-looking."

"Competition?" Potter says. Then he seems to get it. "Oh, are you one of Ava's ex-boyfriends?"

"Her ex-fiancé, actually," Nathaniel says.

There is a beat of silence, during which Ava wants to vaporize. Then she says, "Gibby, you must be freezing. Let's get you inside."

"I'm freezing too," Nathaniel says. "I wonder if Mitzi has made any of her world-famous mulled cider?"

Has Mitzi made any of her Cider of a Thousand Cloves? Why, yes, she has! Mitzi is *thrilled* to see everyone—because what is Christmas without visitors? She hasn't gone so far as to wear her Mrs. Claus dress (Ava thinks she has permanently retired it), but she is wearing a Christmas sweater with a reindeer appliquéd on the front.

"Look who's here!" Mitzi cries out. "It's Potter! And you must be Gibby!" Mitzi gives Gibby a hug. Over Gibby's shoulder, she catches sight of Nathaniel. "Oh, and look... Nathaniel!"

"Hey, Mitzi," Nathaniel says. "I was happy to hear Bart is safe. I prayed for him every day."

"Well, your prayers worked!" Mitzi says. She beams at Nathaniel as if it were in fact his particular prayers that kept Bart alive. Ava rolls her eyes. In the tug-of-war between Nathaniel and Scott, Mitzi was staunchly for Team Nathaniel. When Nathaniel first entered their lives, it was as the carpenter who was building Mitzi's pantry doors, which are still the pride of the kitchen.

"We hear there's cider," Potter says. He's grinning and Ava loves that he isn't letting Nathaniel's presence ruin his evening. He got completely hoodwinked, accepting a ride from Ava's ex-boyfriend—ex-*fiancé*, actually, although they were engaged for all of thirty minutes—and yet he couldn't look happier.

"There's also beer," Ava says quickly. Worse than subjecting Potter to Nathaniel might be subjecting him to Mitzi's cider.

"I most certainly want cider," Nathaniel says.

"Me too," Potter says.

"I'll have a beer," Gibby says.

Smart man, Ava thinks. While she's in the fridge getting Gibby a beer, she pulls out a bottle of chardonnay and pours herself a glass.

"I can't wait for the wedding!" Nathaniel says once they all have drinks. He raises his glass. "Cheers!"

Ava is quick to mobilize Potter and Gibby. She's going to take them to the Castle, she announces, so that Gibby can check in.

"Gibby?" Nathaniel says. "What about you, Potter? Where are you staying?"

Ava glares at Nathaniel. "I think someone left his manners on Block Island."

"I'm staying with Ava," Potter says.

"Good for you, man," Nathaniel says. He finishes his cider and deposits his cup in the sink. There is mistletoe hanging above his head. He looks at the mistletoe, then looks at Ava.

Leave now, Ava thinks. Or he can stay and hang with Mitzi. Ava doesn't care. Doesn't Nathaniel *understand?* She likes *Potter!* She thinks back to the previous December, Stroll weekend, when Nathaniel had returned to Nantucket from the Vineyard and Ava bumped into him at the bar at the Boarding House. He had been relentless then, too, come to think of it, but his persistence had been rewarded. He and Ava had started dating again. Maybe he thinks this time is no different. Ava admires his chutzpah even as she feels sorry for him. This time *is* different.

"Okay, we're off!" Ava says to Mitzi. "We're dropping Gibby at the hotel, then we're going to Nautilus for dinner."

"Be careful in this snow," Mitzi says.

"Nautilus?" Potter says.

"You'll love it," Nathaniel says. "Get the blue-crab fried rice, it's off the chain. Come to think of it, I may go to Nautilus myself. I'll probably see you guys there. I've been missing that rice something fierce."

Ava barely suppresses her smile. She and Potter aren't going to Nautilus. They are going to Fifty-Six Union.

"Bye!" she cries out.

MARGARET

Because she has to button things up before her weeklong vacation and because her new assistant, Jennifer, has yet to develop mind-reading skills, Margaret and Drake don't get on the road until nearly ten o'clock on Thursday night. The West Side Highway is a parking lot. There's an accident at Seventy-Second Street that ties them up for forty-five minutes.

Drake sighs. "Should we just go home and start out in the morning?"

"No," Margaret says. "We have to get to Hyannis tonight."

"Margaret."

"He's my *son*," Margaret says.

"I realize this, Margaret," Drake says. "I was just thinking about... you know, not dying."

Margaret bows her head. She is feeling very uptight and anxious. She gets like this every once in a while. It's not a part of herself that she likes, but it's a part of herself that she acknowledges. She prefers to be in control; situations that are out of her control drive her crazy.

"Please," she says. She reaches out to touch Drake's arm. She loves him so much. She doesn't want to turn into a witch because of Elvira. "Let's try."

Drake straightens up in the driver's seat. "Only for you."

It takes them nearly three hours to reach exit 11 on I-95, Darien, Connecticut. By then, it's a quarter to one in the morning and the road conditions are abysmal and they have seen plenty of accidents and cars abandoned on the side of the highway.

"We're stopping here," Drake says. "There's a Howard Johnson's."

"Drake."

"Margaret."

"I'll drive if you're tired. Let me drive."

"No," Drake says. "The roads aren't safe."

"But—" Margaret says.

"I told you we should have left Wednesday night," Drake says.

"I couldn't!" Margaret says. "I asked and got shot down."

"I understand that, Margaret," Drake says. "But now we have to deal with the consequences. The roads aren't safe. I'm making a unilateral decision here. We are stopping and spending the night at the Howard Johnson's." Drake pulls into the parking lot of the sad little motel decorated in the signature turquoise and orange. Margaret can't believe any Howard Johnson's still exist; this must be the last one left in America. What ever happened to them? Margaret wonders. Would it be worth doing a story on? Maybe a segment for *CBS Sunday Morning*? Howard Johnson's makes Margaret think of vanilla milk shakes and cheese dreams with tomato and bacon. Her stomach grumbles.

"I'll go in," Drake says. "We don't need the front-desk clerk seeing you."

"No," Margaret agrees. She leans back and closes her eyes. She is suddenly exhausted. She can sleep anywhere, even a Howard Johnson's.

A few minutes later, Drake knocks on the window, waking Margaret up.

"There's no room at the inn," he says.

"Seriously?"

"A lot of wayward travelers tonight. Or so says Mrs. Herbert, the battle-ax at the front desk. But I think she was holding out on me, waiting for me to slip her a bribe."

"This place really *is* stuck in the 1950s," Margaret says. She opens the door and steps outside. She sinks in snow up to her knees.

Upon seeing Margaret Quinn walk into the lobby, Mrs. Herbert, of the exit 11 Howard Johnson's, blinks her watery blue eyes behind her glasses.

"Are you—" she says to Margaret.

Margaret puts the very last of the day's energy into giving Mrs. Herbert a smile. "Yes, I am. And I come on bended knee. We need a room, any room."

Sure enough, Mrs. Herbert says, "I do have one room. I musta overlooked it before." She cuts a glance at Drake, then hands him an actual key. The turquoise tag says *room 42.* She softens her expression when she turns back to Margaret. "Do you think I could get an autograph?"

"It would be my pleasure, Mrs. Herbert," Margaret says.

Room 42 has two twin beds, but the sheets are new and the turquoise blanket seems okay. There's a rotary phone on the table between the two beds. Margaret stares at it, wondering if she's dreaming. Then she takes off her boots and lies down. Will Drake get the light? She is asleep before she can even ask.

A phone rings. Margaret jolts awake and reaches for the receiver of the rotary phone.

Dial tone.

No, it's her cell phone. Her cell phone is ringing. Margaret pulls it out from under her pillow. *Please,* she thinks. *Don't let it be a news emergency.*

The display says *Mitzi*. It's twenty after five in the morning.

Kelley? Margaret thinks. Has something happened to Kelley? Margaret is seized by panic. Kelley, her children's father, her partner for half of her adult life, her dearest friend, a man she loves more than she would ever admit. She almost doesn't answer. She can't hear the news. Why else would Mitzi be calling her at five in the morning?

"Hello?" Margaret says.

"Margaret?" Mitzi says. "Did I wake you?"

"Yes," Margaret says. "We stopped in Connecticut. The roads. We're at a…" She can't remember the name of the motel.

But Mitzi doesn't seem to care. "Connecticut?" she says. "That's fantastic! That's perfect!" She calls out, "Kelley, Margaret and Drake are in Connecticut!" There's a pause. "Where in Connecticut?"

Margaret takes a sip of ice water that has been thoughtfully placed next to the rotary phone. "Darien."

"Darien," Mitzi says to Kelley." Then she says, "Can you be in Hartford by eight thirty?"

Margaret and Drake hit the road at six—which is, sadly, too early to enjoy the bacon-and-eggs special on offer at the restaurant. But they can't risk being late.

Bart Quinn is due to land in Hartford at quarter to nine. Logan is closed until at least noon, but Hartford, being farther west and out of the direct path of Elvira, is open. Margaret and Drake are to pick Bart up and drive him to Hyannis, where they will meet up with Paddy, Jennifer, the boys, and Isabelle's parents. They will all take the 2:45 ferry over—assuming the ferry is up and running—and be on Nantucket by five o'clock.

Phew!

The press has gotten wind that five of the missing Marines are landing at Bradley International, and hence, the place is a zoo. Margaret is fairly incognito in sunglasses and a shearling hat but when she needs to slice through the crowd to collect Bart, she takes her glasses off and shakes her famous red hair free of the hat.

A young reporter from WFSB in Hartford turns around, sees Margaret Quinn, and shrieks.

"Oh my goodness," she says. "I can't believe I'm seeing you in person! You are...you are absolutely my hero!"

"I shouldn't be your hero," Margaret says. "He should be." She points to Private Bartholomew James Quinn, Ninth Regiment, First Division, who has just stepped off the passenger ramp into the terminal. Cameras flash and microphones are pushed in his face.

It's Bart. In person. Bart! Margaret feels so humbled, so *honored* to be the one picking him up. She waves and calls out, "Bart!"

"Margaret!" he says. He shakes the hands of his fellow Marines, and then they all salute one another, creating a magnificent photo op, after which he grabs Margaret and gives her a giant bear hug. More flashes go off.

Margaret ushers Drake forward. "Bart, this is my husband, Dr. Drake Carroll."

"Husband?" Bart says. "But you promised to wait for me."

Drake shakes Bart's hand. "Thank you for serving our country, young man," he says. "Thank you for defending our freedom."

"Freedom," Bart says, touching the scar on his face. He looks up at the ceiling; tears seem to be threatening. "Freedom has a whole new meaning now."

JENNIFER

They are on a tight schedule with no margin for error, so even though Paddy is now coming with them—making for an extremely crowded car—Jennifer puts herself in charge. The Beaulieus are to land at Logan from Nova Scotia at twelve thirty, assuming the runways get cleared in time. Jennifer now sees her tax dollars at work. Hundreds of plows are employed all over Boston, digging the city and its residents out.

"The ferry leaves at two forty-five," Jennifer says. "I don't know what Route 3 is going to look like. The Beaulieus will needs to get their luggage, so let's say we hit the road by one. Can we get to Hyannis in an hour and fifteen minutes?"

"I've done it in forty-nine," Patrick says. "But that was in the middle of the night, no traffic, no severe weather conditions."

Forty-nine minutes? It's a miracle Patrick is still alive. Jennifer needs him to be speedy...but safe. She isn't about to become a holiday-driving statistic.

*   *   *

The Beaulieus' plane arrives a little early. *Très bien!* They're standing out in front of Terminal E with their luggage at twelve forty-five. And they've brought only carry-ons. *Magnifique!*

The only problem is the language barrier. Kevin warned Jennifer that the Beaulieus speak no English, none. Meaning Jennifer will have to rely on her four years of high school French.

"Bonjour!" she says. *"Je m'appelle* Jennifer Quinn." She shakes hands with Madame first, a fair beauty like Isabelle with a reserved but elegant smile, and then with Monsieur, who is a large man, hale and hearty. He has black hair with gray at the temples. They are younger than Jennifer expected and chicly dressed. Madame's camel-colored slacks still hold a crease. How is this possible after twenty-four hours of travel, including a night spent in a Canadian airport? Jennifer helps Madame with her carry-on and introduces Paddy and the boys.

"Mon mari, Patrick, *et mes fils,* Barrett, Pierce, *et* Jaime."

The boys have been asked to say *Bonjour* when they meet the Beaulieus, but only Pierce and Jaime comply. Barrett says, *"¡Hola!"*—smart aleck—which makes Monsieur throw his head back and laugh, setting everyone at ease.

"Okay," Jennifer says as they all get in the car, pleased that this part of the plan has gone better than expected. She pulls her seat all the way forward to give Monsieur maximum legroom, then turns to Paddy. "Step on it."

Route 3 isn't bad. It has been plowed and now the sun is out, making the drive very bright.

Jennifer receives a text from Margaret. She and Drake have Bart! They're going to meet them at the steamship at two fifteen. Jennifer tells Patrick this in a low voice. He adjusts his sunglasses and, Jennifer sees, wipes away a tear.

"I'm going to see my brother," Patrick says.

Maybe. Almost immediately, they hit traffic; they slow down, then come to a complete stop.

No! Jennifer thinks. It's one thirty. They really don't have time for this.

Monsieur Beaulieu, definitely the more loquacious of the two, spews forth a bunch of sentences *en français*. Jennifer has no idea what he's saying and she's too tense to try to figure it out.

Madame says, *"Elle ne comprends pas, mon choux."*

"Désolée," Jennifer says. She has a perfectly good *Rosetta Stone French* at home on the library bookshelves, but who has time to relearn a language she was only mediocre at in the first place?

One thirty-five; one forty. Jennifer hates feeling so anxious, but at this point, she's certain they're going to miss the boat. If they do miss it, they'll have to take the eight-fifteen, which doesn't get them to Nantucket until ten thirty. No; unacceptable. And yet, what can Jennifer do? She can't make the hundreds of cars in front of her go any faster.

Or can she? Possibly Jennifer's mental anguish has some real force, because at that second, traffic starts to move and a few moments later, they're flying along.

They cross the Sagamore Bridge at two minutes past two. Margaret texts to say that she and Drake and Bart have just arrived. They're going to park and wait for Paddy and Jennifer outside the terminal.

There's quite a line of cars, Margaret texts. *Do you have a reservation?*

Jennifer had a reservation...on yesterday's boat. With all the excitement, she neglected to call and figure out if her ticket would be valid on this boat; she just assumed it would be. But now she remembers that the steamship has a laundry list of specific rules. Jennifer calls the steamship office in Hyannis. The first time she calls, the line is busy. The second time she calls, she's told her wait time will be fourteen minutes. She groans.

"What's wrong?" Paddy asks. "We're going to make it."

The steamship parking lot is a mob scene. All of the standby lanes are full. Jennifer's heart sinks. She never considered that anyone else might want to *get* to Nantucket for Christmas. She had thought that the islanders would want to *leave* Nantucket so they could visit family in Vermont or Philadelphia.

Jennifer hops out of the car and hurries into the terminal. She sees Margaret and Drake—and Bart. Her heart lifts like a hot-air balloon and tears come to her eyes unbidden.

"Bart!" she says.

"Jenny!" he says. He comes right over to give her a squeeze and she starts to cry for real. Bart Quinn is the only person other than her long-dead grandfather and, occasionally, Patrick whom she's ever allowed to call her Jenny. It's Bart—he's here; he's safe; he's in uniform; he has a dramatic scar on his face; he looks older, more mature. He looks like a man.

She says, "Paddy and the kids are out in the car. I have to go deal with this." She waves the ferry ticket.

"Go," Bart says. "Deal."

There are four people in front of Jennifer in line. All of them want to get their vehicles on this boat.

"The boat is sold out," the ticket man says. He has the thickest New England accent Jennifer has ever heard, and that's saying something because she has heard some doozies. "And there's no space on the eight-fifteen. The next boat with space for vehicles is at nine o'clock tomorrow morning." (*Tamarah mahnin'.*)

Tomorrow morning? Jennifer thinks.

The woman at the front says, "But I have a ticket from yesterday."

"You got a ticket, he's got a ticket, everyone's got a ticket. Doesn't matter. We honor"—*awnah*—"the tickets of people originally scheduled on this boat first. That's policy. Then we honor the tickets of canceled boats."

"Can we go as passengers if there's no room for the cars?" the woman asks.

"Lady, we got half the commonwealth out in that parking lot." *Pawking lawt.* "This boat is sold out. The eight-fifteen has four passenger tickets left. I can sell you those."

The woman's shoulders sag in defeat. "Yes, please."

The man two people in front of Jennifer—bald, with horn-rimmed spectacles—steps out of line and says, "Looks like I'm going to the airport."

Us too, Jennifer thinks. But those planes hold only nine people, and altogether they are...ten. *Well, Paddy can stay behind a few flights,* she thinks.

"The airport is closed until tomorrow," the ticket man says. He delivers this news with a certain relish, as though he's *enjoying* quashing people's hopes and telling them their holiday plans are ruined. A streak of sadism must be a necessary quality for steamship employees. A nice, kind person with feelings couldn't do this job with any efficacy.

The other two people in front of Jennifer, an older woman and a female college student, leave the line. Jennifer steps boldly up and gives the ticket man her most winning smile. "I have a reservation on yesterday's two-forty-five boat, which was canceled," she says. "I think I heard you say that there's no way I can get on this boat."

"You heard correct," the man says. He's overweight with thinning blond hair and florid skin. His name tag says *Walter*.

Waltah, Jennifer thinks.

"So there's nothing I can do?" Jennifer asks. She leans on the desk and smiles wider, thinking she would do anything shy of seducing Walter to get on this boat. "I have my whole family with me because, you see, my brother-in-law Kevin Quinn is getting married. We're a local Nantucket family."

"Mazel tov," Walter says.

"My other brother-in-law, Bart Quinn? He just got back from Afghanistan. He was one of the missing Marines."

"God bless America," Walter says. "Wish I could help you."

"And my mother-in-law? Is Margaret Quinn." Jennifer hates herself for disclosing this piece of information and trading on Margaret's fame, but she is capital-*D* Desperate.

"I don't know any Margaret Quinn," Walter says. He puts a finger to his chin. "Actually, I do know her. I watch Channel Four nights I'm off."

"Great!" Jennifer says, thinking that, once again, Margaret will be their golden ticket.

"But me knowing who Margaret Quinn is doesn't make any more space on this boat. You get me, sweetheart?" He leans his head closer to her as though he's going to impart a secret, maybe another ferry line servicing Nantucket that nobody else knows about or the name of a guy who sells car spaces on the black market. "Your only chance is finding somebody who already has a ticket on this boat and getting that person to switch with you. Maybe you offer a few hundred bucks? Or, since you're local, maybe someone owes you a favor?"

"Right," Jennifer says. "Thank you." She tries to imagine

Paddy and Bart and Margaret wandering through the vehicles, offering bribes.

"Seriously, sweetheart, I seen it happen," Walter says. "And it's the holidays. People are always nicer."

Jennifer buys a ticket for tomorrow's nine o'clock boat and decides to go outside and talk to Paddy. From here, the situation looks dire, and Jennifer feels responsible. She should have dealt with the ticket change right away. She's an idiot!

Jennifer pushes out the door of the terminal just as a woman is pushing another door to come in. Jennifer looks up.

It's Norah.

"Norah!" Jennifer says. She feels caught.

"I've been trying to reach you," Norah says. "Are you going to Nantucket?"

"No," Jennifer says. "It doesn't look like it. My ticket is for yesterday's canceled boat, and this boat is sold out, and the eight-fifteen is sold out. And I have the boys and Margaret and her husband and Bart."

"Bart?" Norah says. "He's home?"

"Just got home," Jennifer says. She throws her hands up and starts to cry. "Or not quite home, I guess." She wipes at her eyes. "Kevin is getting married tomorrow."

"Tomorrow?" Norah says. "Really?"

"Really," Jennifer says. She has now spilled the beans to the only person who shouldn't know. Great. Norah will probably show up and disrupt the proceedings at the moment when people are invited to speak out or forever hold their peace—but Jennifer won't be there to see it because she will still be here in Hyannis. She will be watching the boys ride the carousel at the mall; their Christmas Eve dinner will be at Pizzeria Uno. "I need to get my car on this boat."

"Take my spot," Norah says. "I insist."

"What?" Jennifer says. "You have a spot on this boat?"

"Yes," Norah says. "For my truck. I've been in Boston. I tried to reach you..."

I deleted all your messages, Jennifer thinks.

"If we could take your spot..." Jennifer says.

"It's happening," Norah says. "Let's go switch right now with my buddy Walter."

"Your buddy Walter," Jennifer says.

Walter switches the tickets in a matter of seconds. Jennifer is now on the boat that's about to depart and Norah, using Jennifer's ticket, will be on the nine o'clock the next morning.

Walter says, "Told you, sweetheart. Things like this usually work out. Have a merry Christmas."

"Merry Christmas, Walter," Jennifer says. She turns to Norah. "I don't know how to thank you for this. You are... saving the day. And I mean *really* saving it. Not just for me—for the whole family."

"Tell Kevin I said congratulations," Norah says. "Sincerely. I want him to be happy."

"I'll do that," Jennifer says.

"And that thing I wanted to talk to you about?" Norah says.

"Yes?" Jennifer says. Her stomach tenses as if a punch is coming.

"I'm applying to business schools," Norah says. "I want to go legit, start something real. But I'd like to get an MBA. I was hoping you would write me a letter of recommendation."

Jennifer laughs. A letter of recommendation? *That* is what Norah wanted this whole time? A letter of recommendation for business school?

"I understand if you don't want to..." Norah says.

"Of course I want to!" Jennifer says. "I'd be happy to. I just...well, I thought you wanted to talk about...I don't know...the stuff we were into before."

"I'm finished with all that," Norah says. "Moving onward and upward. But the letter is due January first, so I'll need it next week."

"Consider it done," Jennifer says. She hugs Norah and kisses her cheek. "Merry Christmas, Norah, and thank you."

She hurries out the door with her new ticket and waves at her family. They have a boat to catch.

CHRISTMAS EVE

KEVIN

Later, he will not be able to say how the Siasconset Union Chapel was decorated. (There was an evergreen wreath with a red velvet bow hanging from the end of each pew and, on the altar, two majestic arrangements of red roses, greens, and holly.) He will not remember what music was played. (The church organ was accompanied by cello and trumpet. The Quinns' new friend Gordon Russell sang "O Holy Night" after the vows.) He will not remember what the bridesmaids wore (long red velvet sheaths, slit to the knee) or whether the bow ties were straight or cockeyed on his brothers' tuxedos (Patrick's tie was straight, Bart's cockeyed).

All Kevin will remember is the moment the guests rose and he saw Isabelle Beaulieu standing at the other end of the aisle on the arm of her father, the rather dashing Arnaud Beaulieu. As recently as yesterday, Kevin might have said a wedding was superfluous. He and Isabelle already knew everything about each other; what did a piece of paper matter?

But as she processed toward him wearing a strapless column dress of the whitest silk with a long lace veil, her hair a crown of blond braids, her eyes dewy, her smile shy, it was as though he were seeing her for the first time. He got a lump in his throat.

What in his life had he done to deserve such an enchanting creature? How did he, Kevin Quinn, the middle brother, without the ambition of the older or the bravery of the younger, get so lucky? He had no idea, but he was grateful.

AVA

The wedding is storybook perfect. Sure, the chapel is chilly, but as soon as it fills with people, it warms up. Nathaniel, Ava notices as she starts down the aisle, must have been the last to arrive, or maybe he intentionally chose the back pew so that he would be the first person Ava saw when she processed in. She focuses on her three handsome brothers standing at the altar.

Bart is the tallest of the three, thanks to the genes from Mitzi's father, Joe, who was six foot five. Seeing the three of them standing together registers as completely natural, but it's also surreal. Bart is here. He's right here.

Sitting three rows from the front are Potter and Gibby. Ava saves her best smile for them.

When the ceremony is over and all of the pictures have been taken, Kevin and Isabelle climb into the fire truck with George—who has done a quick change from his coat and tie into his Santa suit—and all the guests cheer and wave. George honks the horn and off they go, husband and wife, Mr. and Mrs. Quinn.

Meanwhile, the inn has been transformed. All of the furniture was moved from the living room to create an open space for mingling that will later serve as a dance floor. Mitzi hired the Four Easy Payments to play, but right now, there is Christmas music piped in. The playlist is a variety of carols rather than just "Joy to the World."

The caterers have laid out a serious spread of cheese and crackers, crudités and dip, sausages and pâtés. Mitzi asked them to make her infamous sugared dates stuffed with peanut butter and, yes, the salted almond pinecone.

Ava and Bart meet in front of the pinecone. Bart scoops up an obscene amount of soft cheese and nuts on a cracker. *It's fine,* Ava thinks. *He needs to fatten up.*

She wants to have a real conversation with him. She wants to ask him what happened, what it was like, how he felt, how he survived. But this isn't the time or the place. This is the time to take a flute of champagne from the server's tray and sing along to "Mistletoe and Holly" with Frank Sinatra.

And apparently, it's also the time to set the record straight once and for all. Because when Ava turns around looking for where Potter has gotten to, she sees Nathaniel headed toward her with some kind of cranberry martini in his hand. He has someone trailing him. It's Scott, who is wearing red corduroy pants embroidered with Santa faces, a white shirt, a black wool blazer, and a red-and-green-tartan bow tie.

"I've brought reinforcements," Nathaniel says. He kisses Ava on the cheek. "You look beautiful, by the way."

"Stunning," Scott says.

Ava glares at Scott. "Where's Mz. Ohhhhhh?"

"She's moving to Newport Beach," he says. "California."

"We came to tell you we don't want you to move to New York," Nathaniel says. "Stay here on Nantucket or come to Block Island. Choose one of us."

Ava feels a hand slip around her waist and she knows it's Potter. She has called in her own reinforcements.

"It's probably good the three of you are here," Ava says. "So all three of you can hear me say this. I am moving to New York to run the music department at the Copper Hill School. That is my reason for moving. But as far as my love life is concerned..." Here, she pauses. Nathaniel and Scott have been so dear to her. She has loved them both for different reasons: Nathaniel is fun-loving and laid-back; Scott is solid and kind with a streak of mischief that appears every once in a while. But neither of them was able to capture Ava's entire heart as Potter has managed to do.

"As far as my love life is concerned, there is only one man I want and that is this man right here, Potter Lyons. So I hope I can keep the two of you as friends and see you when I come home for the summer, but I will never date either of you again and I'm asking you both to respect that."

Nathaniel looks angry; Scott looks morose. Potter lifts Ava's face and—adding insult to injury for the two men—gives Ava the loveliest kiss, possibly of her life. She feels clean and free and honest and empowered. She has come to a decision that makes her feel, well—Ava's eyes linger on the word hanging over the mantel—*joy*.

The Four Easy Payments have set up over by the Christmas tree and now they launch into "Little Saint Nick," by the Beach Boys. Nathaniel is the first to reach over and shake Potter's hand. Scott follows suit and says, "Take good care of her, man."

"She can take care of herself," Potter says. "I'm just going to love her."

Nathaniel looks at Scott. "Drink?" he says.

"Heck, yeah," Scott says, and the two head to the bar.

Potter turns to Ava. "Dance?"

"I thought you'd never ask," she says.

KELLEY

He should have been the happiest man alive, but he simply doesn't feel well. His head aches, there's a loud buzzing in his left ear, and splotches are appearing in front of him—there are amorphous blue blobs in the upper right corner of his vision. He can see the party is a raging success. Ava and Potter are dancing; so is Isabelle and her father, Kevin and Margaret, Patrick and Madame Beaulieu, Jennifer and Drake, and George and Mary Rose—who, Kelley has just found out, have gotten engaged. Bart is busy charming Mrs. Gabler, his old kindergarten teacher, who must think better of him now that he is a war hero. Kelley watches as Mitzi saves him, pulling Bart onto the dance floor. Kelley has always been mesmerized by Mitzi's beauty—quirky though it is—but he can honestly say that he has never seen Mitzi look as luminous as she does tonight. She has her son back. Kelley is sure nothing else will ever matter as much.

They aren't following any kind of usual wedding protocol, although when this song ends, Kelley will saber the champagne as he does every year on Christmas Eve, and then Kevin and Isabelle will dance to "The Christmas Song."

Kelley gets ready. He pulls the magnum of Taittinger out of the ice and finds his saber. Then he signals the bandleader, who ends the song and says, "Ladies and gentlemen, our gracious host, Kelley Quinn, will now saber the champagne."

The crowd cheers, Monsieur Beaulieu is especially enthusiastic—probably because he's French. Kelley worries he'll fumble the ball somehow; there are a million ways to screw up a sabering even under the best of circumstances, never mind when one is afflicted with brain cancer.

Kelley opens the front door of the inn. Out on Winter Street, the scene is tranquil: snow, streetlights, the neighbors' antique homes buttoned up and quiet. Kelley finds the spot on the neck of the bottle that he must hit just so, and he drags the back of the saber against it.

Kelley turns to the crowd. He focuses on Mitzi's face, a beacon. She winks at him. The wink is like magic; immediately, Kelley feels thirty-nine again. He is dating the roller-disco queen of King of Prussia, Pennsylvania. He is virile, strong, confident. He can do this.

In one fluid motion, Kelley slices off the top of the bottle. The crowd cheers. A server hands Kelley a flute that Kelley fills and then raises to the crowd.

"To Kevin and Isabelle. May they carry the love and the joy of this evening in their hearts for all the days of their marriage. God bless us, every one."

The bandleader sings, " 'Chestnuts roasting on an open fire,' " and the guests form a ring around the floor while Kevin and Isabelle have their first dance. The first of many, many dances, Kelley hopes.

His work is done, he thinks. And now, he must lie down.

He can hear the party continuing on the other side of his closed bedroom door, but within minutes of lying down in the dark, Kelley is transported elsewhere.

The year is 1958. Kelley is six years old. He lives with his parents in Perrysburg, Ohio. His father works for Owens

Corning; they have had a good year. Kelley and his brother, Avery, tiptoe down the stairs on Christmas morning to find that Santa has left them bicycles—a red two-wheeler with training wheels for Kelley and a blue tricycle for Avery. Kelley had sat on Santa's lap at Lasalle and Koch in Toledo the week before, but he had been too shy to ask for a bike and so he'd said he wanted candy and the board game Monopoly.

In his stocking, Kelley finds candy canes, chocolates wrapped in foil, ribbon candy, sugared orange slices, licorice sticks, jelly beans, caramels, root beer barrels, butterscotch drops, Mary Janes, and Necco wafers. And under the tree is a long, flat box that turns out to be … Monopoly.

Santa is real!

It's 1963. The president has been dead for two weeks. Kelley's mother, Frances Quinn, is in mourning and says she doesn't want to celebrate Christmas. Kelley can't stand to think of his little brother, Avery, going without Christmas, so he takes over Matt Zacchio's paper route for two weeks. Perrysburg is experiencing subfreezing temperatures and Matt is eager to hand the route over temporarily. Kelley makes thirty dollars and buys Avery what looks like a briefcase, but when the case is opened, it reveals art supplies: colored pencils, crayons, markers, pastels, and paints with different-size horsehair brushes. For the first time, Kelley understands what is meant by the saying "It is better to give than to receive."

On Christmas morning, Kelley and Avery tiptoe down the stairs to find a wire crate in front of the fire. In the crate is a black Labrador puppy.

A puppy!

They name him Jack, after the late president, and the whole family is cheered, even Frances.

Santa is real!

*   *   *

It's 1971. Kelley and Avery are teenagers. On Christmas Eve, they climb out onto the roof under their dormer window and share a joint. Avery sings "Joy to the World"—the Three Dog Night version. *Jeremiah was a bullfrog.* He is a great singer, and a star athlete as well. His grades put Kelley's to shame. Kelley should hate him, but he doesn't. He loves his brother with all his heart.

In the morning, they sleep in. In fact, Frances has to rap on their bedroom door to wake them. Presents have ceased to matter. What Kelley really wants is a bong, but he can hardly ask his parents for that and, as it turns out, Santa isn't real.

But their mother is real and she has made eggs Benedict and eggnog French toast, she tells them. Because it's Christmas, she says, she warmed the syrup and doubled up on the hollandaise.

Kelley and Avery race each other down the stairs.

It's 1977 and Kelley and Margaret have a baby. They dress him up in a tiny Santa suit and stick him in the baby swing while they make Golden Dreams. The Golden Dream is a cocktail recipe Margaret found in *Good Housekeeping*. She wants to drink them every Christmas, she says. They're a family now. They need traditions.

It's 1986 and Kelley and Margaret have two little boys and a brand-new baby girl. Ronald Reagan is Santa Claus. Kelley is making a fortune trading petroleum futures. He and Margaret are able to buy a brownstone on East Eighty-Eighth Street, eighty-four blocks north of the brownstone Avery bought the year before with his partner, Marcus.

On Christmas, Kelley presents Margaret with a Cartier tank watch.

"This is too extravagant," Margaret says.

"No," Kelley says. " 'Too extravagant' are the guys on the trading floor who go to Norma's for breakfast and order the zillion-dollar omelet."

"But this house is my present," Margaret says.

"This house is our shelter," Kelley says. "The watch is for you. You have put your career on hold in order to give me all of these beautiful, healthy children, including our new princess."

He fastens the watch onto Margaret's wrist.

"I'll never take it off," she says.

It's 1987 and the stock market has just crashed. Kelley knows two men who have killed themselves in the past month. Kelley wanted to give Margaret carte blanche to decorate the brownstone with a real interior designer but now he thinks they'd better save their money.

They buy the boys a Nintendo, and Ava gets every shiny, beeping, talking toy that Fisher-Price makes. They decide they won't buy gifts for each other. But they do have Golden Dreams.

It's 1993 and Kelley can feel his marriage unraveling. How this happened, he isn't quite sure. Work is killing him; he has to do twice as much to make the same money. He has to stay awake to watch the overseas market, so he has a coke habit, just like everyone else in his firm.

As the kids get older, there are bills, bills, and more bills: private school for the boys, a piano teacher for Ava. Margaret wants to work full-time but if she does that, who will run the household and care for the children? They are not getting a nanny. Kelley was raised by his mother, and his children will be raised by their mother. When Margaret calls him a chauvinist and a dinosaur, he goes to the office.

To cover for the dismal state of his marriage, Kelley suggests spending Christmas at Round Hill in Jamaica. It turns out to be seven days of heaven. They have a villa with its own pool; they eat jerk chicken and listen to reggae and do the limbo on the beach. Margaret and Kelley substitute rum punch for the Golden Dreams. Traditions are made to be broken, Kelley says.

It's 2001 and the world has forever changed. The towers have come down; air travel will never feel safe again; Bush has declared war on Afghanistan.

Bart is five years old, a student at the Children's House of Nantucket, a Montessori program where sharing is not required. If Bart is working on something—everything is called work at Montessori—and he doesn't want to be interrupted by another child, he has been taught to say "Maybe another day."

Bart uses this phrase at home any time he wants to be defiant. On Christmas Eve when Kelley and Mitzi dress him up for five o'clock Mass, he says, "Maybe another day." When they tell him to finish his steamed snow peas, he says, "Maybe another day." When they try to put him to bed early because Santa is coming, he says, "Maybe another day."

Ava is sixteen. She doesn't like Bart to bother her when she's playing the piano because he bangs the keys. But on Christmas, she lets him lean against her as she plays "O Little Town of Bethlehem" and "Silent Night." He falls asleep in her lap as she plays "Away in a Manger," and Mitzi carries him to bed.

It's 2010, the afternoon of Christmas Eve, and Kelley has accompanied some guests of the inn to the red-ticket drawing in town. It's a Nantucket tradition, but Mitzi has just announced that she hates it. She finds it mercenary, a huge crowd gathering on Main Street . . . why? To see if they've won money. She's going to stay home instead and have a cup of tea with George the Santa Claus, she says.

Kelley points out that it's a Chamber of Commerce function and they are members, so he's going to represent. He also has four pockets filled with red tickets and he's not going to lie—he would love to be the five-thousand-dollar winner. The inn is losing money every minute. Even a thousand dollars would help. If they call his name, he vows he will donate 10 percent to the Nantucket Food Pantry.

He doesn't win but nevertheless, the gathering is festive, primarily because he bumps into Fast Eddie Pancik on the street, and he lets Kelley nip from his flask.

When Kelley gets home, warmed by the whiskey and the holiday cheer, he can't find Mitzi. She's not in the kitchen preparing for their now-annual Christmas Eve soiree, and she's not in the bedroom getting ready. He calls out for her. Nothing. Her car is still in the driveway. She's in the inn somewhere.

He finds her rushing down the back stairway in her Mrs. Claus dress and high black suede boots. She looks flushed.

"Where have you been?" he asks.

"Me?" she says. "Nowhere."

Kelley wakes up with a start.

He's still alive—good. There was something life-passing-before-his-eyes about the dreams he was just having. He should never have invoked *A Christmas Carol* during his toast. He must have awoken the Ghost of Christmas Past.

The bedroom is dark; the house quiet. Is the party over? Yes, Mitzi is asleep next to him, her breathing steady and deep.

Kelley needs his pain meds and a large glass of ice water. Gingerly, he gets to his feet. He's still in his tuxedo, minus his shoes, jacket, and tie.

He tiptoes out into the hallway, remembering himself and
Avery so many years ago.

The party has been cleaned up, the furniture returned to
its usual spots. That must have taken a lot of people a bunch
of time, and Kelley feels guilty for not helping. He'll make it
up to everyone in the morning by cooking a big breakfast: a
cheese strata, bacon and sausage; blueberry cornmeal pancakes; eggnog French toast; fresh-squeezed juice; and, of
course, Golden Dreams.

"Dad?"

Kelley jumps. Bart is sitting by himself on the sofa with
Mitzi's military-man nutcracker on the coffee table in front
of him. There is still a log burning in the fireplace, but the
only other light comes from the twinkling tree and the letters *J-O-Y* glowing over the mantel.

Kelley sits down on the sofa, then realizes that Bart is
crying.

"Dad," Bart says again, but his voice breaks.

"I know you're a big man now," Kelley says. "But I hope
you're not too old to let your dad hold you." He opens his
arms and Bart crawls into them, just as he used to when he
was a little boy, ruined by Montessori. He cries against Kelley's chest and Kelley rubs his son's back. God only knows
what he's been through, what he's seen; brothers in arms
killed, for certain, and maybe worse. It'll all come out—but
not right now. Now, Bart needs good old-fashioned comfort.
Eventually, his cries subside; he wipes his face on the bottom of Kelley's tuxedo shirt.

"What's going on out here?"

Kelley half turns his head and beckons with his free arm
for Mitzi to join them. She settles on the other side of Bart
and the three of them grasp one another.

Kelley remembers a crèche that his mother used to have,

with painted figurines and a manger with a thatched roof. Kelley and Avery used to set it up each year: shepherds, wise men, cows, sheep, goats, the Holy Family, and the angel, who hung on a hook at the peak of the roof.

As he and Mitzi cradle Bart, Kelley thinks about how Joseph and Mary must have felt on the original Christmas night. The word illuminated in front of Kelley is *joy,* but what Kelley feels is something more profound. It is, perhaps, the oldest and purest of all Christmas emotions.

Wonder.

January 1, 2017

Dear Family and Friends,

I apologize for the tardiness of this holiday letter. As you will soon understand, the past year has been chock-full of news, so many dramatic developments that instead of a letter, I should be writing a novel.

Kelley stops typing and stares at the screen. He *should* write a novel. Is that the best idea he's ever had, or the worst? He can't tell. It's January first; people all across America are making resolutions: lose weight, spend less time on the phone and more time with the kids, make one new dish per week, enhance vocabulary, volunteer, clean and organize the garage, lose weight, investigate the family's genealogy, go green, save money, lose weight.

Kelley makes a resolution. He is going to write a novel.

And forget the Christmas letter! He's going to start right now, this instant.

He doesn't have any time to waste.

ACKNOWLEDGMENTS

This book is for my brother Doug, who makes a fictional cameo appearance as Dougie Clarence, the CBS meteorologist. Just as I have wanted to be a writer since I learned the alphabet, Doug always dreamed of becoming a weatherman. He presently works as a meteorologist for the National Weather Service in the office of communications and he was instrumental in explaining the science behind a winter storm.

I was lucky enough to have a member of the U.S. Marine Corps describe in colorful detail what he endured to become a Marine, and although he preferred to not be identified by name, I thank him and every single other serviceman and -woman of this great country. God bless America. My heart goes out to the parents of these brave young men and women.

It pains me to have finished with my beloved Quinn family, but to all of you readers who steadfastly followed me from the crystalline days of summer into the *crazed* holiday season and fell in love with these characters as much as I did: *thank you.*

And finally to you, Nantucket Island, forever my muse. You are beautiful at every time of year. No matter how far afield I travel, real joy is always found in coming home.

WINTER STORMS

Questions and Topics for Discussion

1. A variety of beginnings and endings—of relationships, marriages, businesses, and even a prison sentence—play major roles in *Winter Storms*. In what ways are the Quinn family's feelings about these two different stages of life similar? In what ways are they different?

2. If you were in Ava's shoes, which of her suitors would you choose? Have you ever been in a similar romantic predicament?

3. In what ways does Kevin's new business give his life renewed purpose? How are his achievements on his own different from his involvement with the Winter Street Inn?

4. Mitzi, Kelley, and the rest of the Quinns spend a great deal of time waiting for news about Bart. Do you think the Quinns effectively balanced living their own lives with a respect for Bart while waiting for news of his fate? Have you ever had a similar experience when you were waiting for news of a loved one?

5. How does being stranded with their fellow family members during a snowstorm force the Quinns to deal with family resentments they may otherwise have attempted to ignore? Have you ever found yourself "trapped" with your family, and how did you handle it?

ABOUT THE AUTHOR

Elin Hilderbrand's favorite things about winter on Nantucket are seeing the first snowfall of the year on Main Street, watching her three children play basketball, and getting good seats for Christmas Eve Mass at St. Mary's. She wishes the most joyous of holidays to all her readers and gratitude to those who followed her into a different time of the year. *Winter Storms* is her eighteenth novel and the third book in the Winter Street series.

...AND HER NEXT WINTER STREET NOVEL

Book one more stay with the Quinns at the Winter Street Inn in *Winter Solstice*, the heartwarming conclusion to Elin Hilderbrand's bestselling series. Following is an excerpt from the novel's opening pages.

BART

The party is his mother's idea. Bart's birthday is October 31, which is one of the three worst birthdays a person can have, along with Christmas and September 11. It was especially soul crushing when Bart was growing up. Nobody wanted to celebrate a birthday when there was free candy to be had on the street just by dressing up and knocking on doors.

Bart agrees to the party, reluctantly, but he lays down some rules. Mitzi is sitting on the end of Bart's bed in Bart's room with her pen and her legal pad, ready to plan. Does she notice that the room smells strongly of marijuana smoke? She must, though she doesn't comment. Bart figures one reason she wants to throw a party is so Bart will get up out of bed. So he will be social, interact, return to the fun-loving idiot he used to be. He has been back from Afghanistan for ten months, and what Mitzi doesn't seem to understand is that the person Bart used to be...is gone.

"No costumes," Bart says. "Since you're all keen to write things down, start with that."

The corners of Mitzi's mouth droop. Bart doesn't want to make his mother any sadder than she already is, but on this he must hold firm. No costumes.

"Write it down," he says again.

"But . . . ," Mitzi says.

Bart closes his eyes against his frustration. This is Mitzi, he reminds himself. Once she gets an idea, it's nearly impossible to reason with her. Bart tries imagining what a costume party thrown by the Quinn family might look like: His brother Patrick can come wearing an orange jumpsuit and handcuffs, since he spent eighteen months in prison for insider trading while Bart was gone. Bart's brother Kevin can wear a beret and kerchief, and carry a baguette under one arm. Since marrying Isabelle—who was a chambermaid and breakfast cook when Bart left—Kevin has become a regular Charles de Gaulle. Once, when Bart visited Kevin and Isabelle's new house—there had been talk of Bart moving in with them and serving as a manny to their daughter, Genevieve, and brand-new infant son, KJ, but no, sorry, Bart isn't good with children—Bart heard Kevin singing in French to his newborn son.

Singing in French!

Ava can come dressed as a femme fatale in a black dress with a plunging neckline, smoking a cigarette in one of those old-fashioned holders since apparently she has become quite the temptress in the past three years. She tried to explain the trajectory of her love life to Bart—Nathaniel, then Scott, then Nathaniel *and* Scott, then she was, ever so briefly, *engaged* to Nathaniel, then Nathaniel took a job on Block Island, so she was back with Scott. Then Scott got one of the teachers at the high school pregnant, and Ava was left with no one for a matter of months. And somewhere in there— Bart can't remember, his brain has more holes than Swiss cheese now—she met a third person, Potter Lyons, or maybe it's Lyons Potter, who is a professor somewhere in New York City, but according to Ava, Potter Lyons or Lyons Potter is *not* the reason Ava now lives on the Upper East Side of New

York and teaches music at a fancy private school where her students include the grandson of Quincy Jones and two of Harrison Ford's nieces. Ava has grown up. It's a good thing, a natural thing, Bart realizes—but still, he feels resentful. Who is supposed to hold the family together with Ava gone? Certainly not Bart.

And what about a costume for Bart's father, Kelley? Kelley has brain cancer, and after enduring fifteen more rounds of chemo and twenty-eight rounds of radiation, he made an executive decision: no more treatment. For a few months it looked like maybe he had beaten back the disease enough to eke out a few more good years. This past summer he was still able to flip the blueberry cornmeal pancakes and serve the guests breakfast with a smile. He and Mitzi were still walking every day from Fat Ladies Beach to Cisco and back again. But then, in mid-September, while Kelley and Bart were watching the University of Tennessee play Ole Miss— Bart's closest friend in the platoon, Centaur, now dead, had been a huge Vols fan, and Bart had vowed to watch the team since Centaur no longer could—Kelley suffered a seizure and lost sight in his left eye. Now, a mere four weeks later, he is relegated to a wheelchair, and Mitzi has called hospice.

Kelley is beyond the point of dressing up, and that's the real reason Bart doesn't want costumes. Kelley is going to die.

When Bart was on the plane home from Iceland, he swore that he would never let anything bother him again. But returning home to news of his father's cancer had cut Bart out at the knees. Along with profound sadness, he feels cheated. He managed to stay alive and make it home despite untold horrors; it's not fair that Kelley is now dying. Kelley won't be around to see Bart get married or have children. He won't know if Bart makes a success of himself or not. It taps into Bart's oldest resentment: Bart's three older siblings have gotten a lot more of Kelley than Bart has. They've gotten the best of him, and Bart, the sole child from Kelley's marriage to Mitzi, has had to make do with what was left over.

Mitzi winds one of her curls around her finger. "What if we compromise?" she asks. "What if I say 'Costumes optional'? I have an outfit I really want to wear."

Bart closes his eyes. He envisions some guests wearing costumes and some wearing regular clothes. The party will look like a half-eaten sandwich. He debates giving in to Mitzi just to make her happy and to prove himself a nice, reasonable guy—but he can't seem to buck his absolute hatred of Halloween.

"No costumes," he says. "Please, Mom. You can throw the party, I'll go and try to have a good time. But no costumes."

Mitzi sighs, then stands to leave the room. "You could use an air freshener in here," she says.

Bart gives her half a smile, the most he can muster. It's only after Mitzi walks out, closing the door behind her, that he realizes she didn't actually concede.

EDDIE

It's the first invitation he has received since he got out of jail, and Eddie won't lie: he's over the moon. Eddie Pancik, formerly known as Fast Eddie, dutifully served a three-to-five-year sentence (in two years and three months) at MCI–Plymouth for conspiracy and racketeering after confessing to pimping out his crew of Russian cleaning girls to his high-end real estate clients. Eddie's conviction had coincided with his discovery that his wife, Grace, was having an affair with their handsome and handsomely paid landscape architect, Benton Coe—and so when Eddie had first gotten to jail, it had felt like his world was caving in.

If Eddie learned anything while being incarcerated, it's that human beings are resilient. He won't say he *thrived* during his time at MCI–Plymouth, but it wasn't nearly as awful as he'd expected. In some ways he appreciated the discipline and the hiatus from the rat race. Whereas before, Eddie's focus had always been on drumming up business and the next big deal, jail taught him to be mindful and present. He went to the weight room every day at seven a.m., then to breakfast, then he spent the morning teaching an ersatz real estate class in the prison library. The clientele of the prison was primarily white-collar criminals—embezzlers, credit card scammers, some drug lords but none with violent convictions—and nearly all of them, Eddie found, had a good head for business. Most times Eddie's "classes" turned into roundtable discussions of how good business ideas went awry. Sometimes the line was blurry, they all agreed.

Eddie even managed to sell a house while in lockup—to a man named Forrest Landry, who had hundreds of millions in trust with his wife, Karen. Karen Landry was one of those long-suffering types—Forrest had been unfaithful to her as well as to the law—but prison had made Forrest penitent, and he decided that a house on the platinum stretch of Hulbert Avenue would be just the thing to make amends.

He paid the listing price: $11.5 million.

Eddie's commission was $345,000. Eddie's sister, Barbie, acted as Eddie's proxy, and the windfall was directed to Eddie's wife, Grace, who used the money to pay college tuition for their twin daughters, Hope and Allegra. Hope had gotten into every college she applied to and had opted to go to Bucknell University in the middle of Exactly Nowhere, Pennsylvania. The school is ridiculously expensive, although—as Hope pointed out—*not* as expensive as Duke, USC, or Brown, her other three choices. She is getting straight As and playing the flute in a jazz band. Now in the fall of her sophomore year, she's even pledging a sorority, Alpha Delta Pi, which both Eddie and Grace agreed was a good thing, as Hope had been a bit of a loner in high school.

Allegra didn't get in anywhere except UMass Dartmouth and Plymouth State because of poor test scores and even worse grades. She decided on UMass Dartmouth, with an eye to transferring to the main campus in Amherst her sophomore year—but instead she flunked out. She returned to Nantucket and went to work for her aunt Barbie at Bayberry Properties, a company owned by Barbie's husband, Glenn Daley.

Eddie is secretly okay with the fact that Allegra isn't in college, and not just for the obvious financial reasons. Eddie sees a lot of himself in Allegra. He, too, struggled with traditional book learning. Allegra has common sense, ambition, and enviable social skills. She has started out as the receptionist at Bayberry Properties, but Glenn has been talking about promoting her to office manager sometime in the next year. From there it will only be a matter of time before she pursues her broker's license. The kid is going to be a success; Eddie is sure of it. He has seen her in action at the office— she is polite, professional, and confident way beyond her years. She's even nice on the phone when the odious Rachel McMann calls. Rachel used to work at Bayberry Properties, but while Eddie was in jail, she struck out on her own, and she's had an alarming amount of success, even though she's the worst gossip on the island.

Glenn Daley, once Eddie's biggest rival, offered Eddie a desk at Bayberry Properties at Barbie's insistence. Eddie now sits in the back row against the wall with two other first-year associates, and the three of them split phone duty, although somehow Eddie always ends up getting stuck with the weekend shifts. It's like starting in the business all over again, but Eddie tries to feel grateful. He should be humbled that Glenn Daley has chosen to claim his convicted felon of a brother-in-law and give him a fresh start.